Beneath The Ashes A Testament of Faith

Nazreen zainab

Published by Nazreen zainab, 2024.

This is a work of fiction. Similarities to real people, places, or events are entirely coincidental.

BENEATH THE ASHES A TESTAMENT OF FAITH

First edition. September 14, 2024.

ISBN: 979-8227226938

Written by Nazreen zainab.

Also by Nazreen zainab

Deception in Bloom
Beneath The Ashes A Testament of Faith
Resilience In The Shadows

Table of Contents

To the resilient souls who have endured the unimaginable, yet
still rise with grace and strength.

To the people of Palestine, whose unwavering faith lights even
the darkest of days.

And to every heart that holds onto hope when the world
seems determined to take it away this story is for you. May you
always find light, even beneath the ashes.

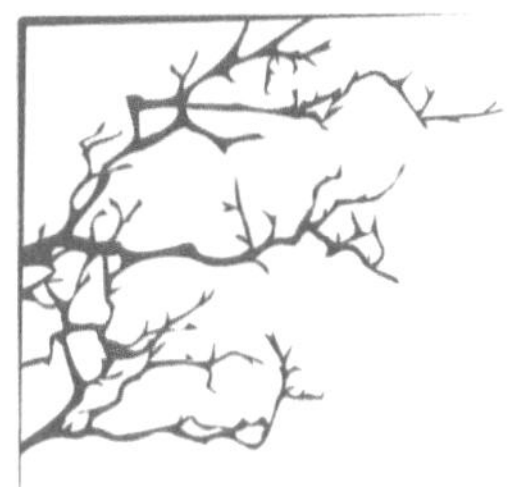

Prologue

A Beautiful Day in Gaza

It was a day like any other in Gaza, a day that began with the soft hues of dawn spilling over the horizon, turning the sky into a canvas of pinks and oranges. The morning air was cool and crisp, carrying with it the scent of the sea that lapped against the shores just beyond the city's edge. Birds chirped in the palm trees that lined the narrow streets, their songs blending with the distant hum of the bustling market that was beginning to wake.

In the heart of the city, nestled among the narrow alleys and stone buildings, stood a small, modest coffee shop. Its walls were worn from years of salty breezes and sun, yet the place exuded a warmth and charm that made it a beloved spot for the locals. The sign above the door read "Al-Amal," which meant "hope" in Arabic—a fitting name, given the comfort it brought to everyone who passed through its doors.

Inside, the air was thick with the rich aroma of freshly brewed coffee, mingling with the scent of sweet pastries just out of the oven. The coffee shop had been in the family for generations, passed down from father to son, and now to daughter. This was where the main character, Yasmin, found her purpose each day, helping her father run the business that was both their livelihood and their pride.

Yasmin was in her early twenties, a young woman with striking features—a cascade of dark, wavy hair that she often tucked beneath a modest headscarf, eyes the colour of the Mediterranean Sea, and a smile that could light up even the darkest of days. She had grown up in this coffee shop, learning the art of brewing the perfect cup of coffee, understanding the subtleties of the spices that flavoured their most popular dishes, and mastering the delicate balance between sweet and savoury in their beloved desserts.

Her elder brother, Omar, worked alongside her. Omar was tall and strong, with a quiet demeanour that belied his deep love for his family. He had always been the protector, the one who would do anything to keep his siblings safe. Yasmin admired him greatly; he was not just her brother, but her best friend, her confidant.

Two younger brothers, Hassan and Khaled, often ran through the shop, their laughter filling the air as they chased each other between the tables. Hassan, at twelve, was serious for his age, already showing signs of the responsibility that would one day fall upon his shoulders. Khaled, only eight, was a bundle of energy and mischief, always finding ways to make everyone laugh, even on the hardest days. Yasmin adored them both, though she often found herself playing the role of the stern older sister, reminding them to finish their homework or help with the chores.

And then there was Aaliyah , the newest addition to the family. She was a tiny thing, just a few months old, with big, curious eyes that seemed to take in everything around her. Aaliyah was the light of the family, her presence a constant reminder of the beauty of life, even in a place as tumultuous as Gaza. Yasmin would often hold her in her arms, rocking her gently as she hummed old lullabies, dreaming of a future where Aaliyah could grow up in peace.

The coffee shop was bustling with the morning rush. Regular customers, men and women from the neighbourhood, filed in to grab a quick breakfast or linger over a cup of coffee before heading to work. Yasmin moved gracefully behind the counter, her hands working with the speed and precision that came from years of practice. She greeted everyone with a smile, exchanging pleasantries as she poured coffee, served pastries, and made sure every customer felt like family.

"Yasmin, we're running low on sugar," her father, Abbas, called out from the back of the shop. He was a man in his sixties, with greying hair and a kind face that had weathered the years with grace. Despite his age, Abbas was still as sharp and capable as ever, overseeing the shop with the same dedication he had always shown.

"I'll pick some up from the market later," Yasmin replied, already making a mental note of the other supplies they needed. The market was just a few blocks away, a lively place where vendors sold everything from fresh produce to handmade goods. Yasmin loved the market, loved the way it pulsed with life and energy, a stark contrast to the quieter streets around it.

Omar appeared beside her, carrying a tray of freshly baked bread. "Here, let me take over for a while. You've been on your feet since dawn."

Yasmin shook her head, smiling at her brother's concern. "I'm fine, Omar. Besides, the customers seem to like my coffee better than yours," she teased, her eyes sparkling with mischief.

Omar chuckled, a rare sound that always warmed Yasmin's heart. "You might be right about that. But seriously, take a break. I can handle things here."

Reluctantly, Yasmin agreed, stepping out from behind the counter and wiping her hands on her apron. She made her way to the back of the shop, where a small courtyard offered a brief escape from the busyness inside. The courtyard was her favorited part of the coffee shop—a little oasis of green in the midst of the city. Potted plants lined the walls, and a small fountain gurgled softly in the center, its water sparkling in the morning light.

Yasmin sat on a bench beneath a flowering vine, closing her eyes and breathing in the scent of jasmine that filled the air. For a moment, she allowed herself to relax, to forget about the demands of the day and simply enjoy the peace of the morning.

But even as she sat there, a shadow crossed her mind. It was a feeling she couldn't quite shake, a sense that something was about to change. Gaza had always been a place of unrest, of uncertainty. The past few years had been relatively calm, but everyone knew how quickly that could change. There were rumours, whispers of conflict brewing just beyond the horizon. Yasmin tried not to think about it, tried to focus on the here and now, but the thought lingered at the back of her mind, like a storm cloud on the edge of a clear sky.

She was pulled from her thoughts by the sound of footsteps. Omar had come to join her, a cup of coffee in hand. He offered it to her with a smile, and she accepted gratefully.

"Thank you, Omar. I needed this," she said, taking a sip of the rich, dark brew. It was perfect, as always—strong and comforting, with just a hint of sweetness.

Omar sat beside her, his expression thoughtful. "It's quiet today," he remarked, his voice low. "Too quiet."

Yasmin glanced at him, noting the worry in his eyes. "You're thinking about the rumours, aren't you?"

He nodded. "I can't help it. Things have been too calm lately. I keep waiting for the other shoe to drop."

Yasmin reached out, placing a hand on his arm. "We can't live in fear, Omar. We have to keep going, keep living our lives. That's all we can do."

Omar sighed, running a hand through his hair. "I know. But I worry about you, about all of us. I just want to keep you safe."

Yasmin smiled, her heart swelling with love for her brother. "You've always been our protector, Omar. But you can't do it alone. We have to trust in Allah, and in each other."

He looked at her then, his expression softening. "You're right, as always. I just wish I could do more."

Yasmin squeezed his arm gently. "You're doing enough, Omar. We all are."

They sat in silence for a while, sipping their coffee and listening to the sounds of the city waking up around them. Despite the undercurrent of tension, there was still beauty in the world, still moments of peace to be found in the midst of uncertainty.

As the sun climbed higher in the sky, Yasmin knew it was time to return to the coffee shop. The day was just beginning, and there was work to be done. She stood, stretching her arms above her head before turning to her brother.

"Come on, Omar. We've got a business to run," she said, her tone light and playful.

Omar chuckled, standing as well. "Yes, boss," he teased, falling into step beside her as they made their way back inside.

The coffee shop was busier now, with more customers filtering in, their conversations filling the air with a pleasant hum. Yasmin slipped back behind the counter, greeting the regulars with a smile and a nod. Despite the worries that lingered at the edges of her mind, she felt a deep sense of contentment. This was her home, her family, her life. And no matter what the future held, she would cherish these moments, these simple, beautiful moments, for as long as she could.

But the storm was coming, and deep down, Yasmin knew that this peace wouldn't last forever. In Gaza, nothing ever did.

Yet, as she looked out at the faces of the people she loved, she held onto hope. Hope that they would endure, that they would survive whatever was to come. And in that hope, she found strength.

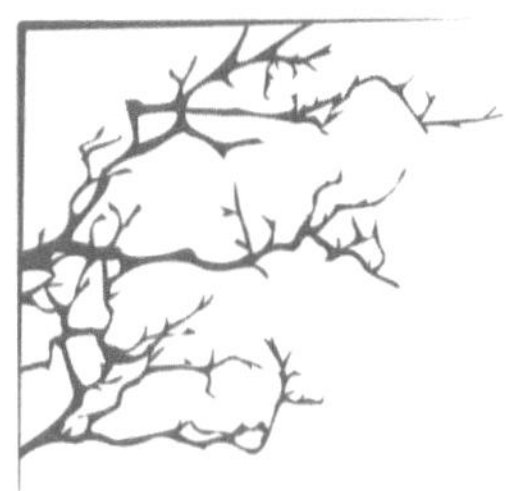

Chapter 1

The Shadow of War

I t started with whispers.............

At first, it was just background noise, the kind of idle talk that passed through the coffee shop with the morning breeze. People mentioned skirmishes along the border, rumours of increased military presence, and murmurings of political tension that never seemed to fade completely from life in Gaza. But no one seemed truly alarmed—not yet. Conflict, after all, had long been a part of their lives. It was always there, lurking beneath the surface of their daily routines, but they had learned to live with it, to go on with their lives despite it.

Yasmin noticed it first in the eyes of the customers who came in for their morning coffee. Where there was once laughter and light-hearted conversation, there was now a heaviness, an unspoken tension that made people glance over their shoulders, their voices lower, more cautious. They gathered in small groups at the tables, sipping their coffee as if it were a shield against the uncertainty that seemed to be creeping in from the edges of their world.

The radio, always playing softly in the background of the shop, began to broadcast more alarming reports. Government officials warned of rising tensions with Israel, and there were rumours of impending military action. There had been airstrikes before, but this time felt different. There was something more serious in the tone of the news anchors, something that made Yasmin pause in the middle of her work to listen more closely. Her hands stilled over the counter as she heard the words "escalation" and "possible invasion," words that sent a chill down her spine despite the warmth of the day.

"Do you think it's true?" asked Zaynab, one of the regular customer who had taken her usual spot near the window. Her voice trembled slightly as she looked up from her cup, her eyes wide with worry.

Yasmin gave a small, tight smile, trying to ease her customer's fears, even though she wasn't sure of the answer herself. "It's hard to say. They've been saying things like this for years. Inshallah, it will pass like before."

But Zaynab didn't look convinced. "My cousin said they've seen more soldiers at the checkpoints. And my brother... he says they've been hearing explosions at night."

Yasmin's heart clenched at the mention of explosions, but she kept her expression calm. "We have to keep faith," she said gently. "Allah will protect us. We can't live in fear every day."

Still, after Zaynab left, Yasmin found herself standing by the window, her gaze drifting out toward the street. The air outside seemed thicker, heavier than it had in the past few weeks. It was as if the whole city was holding its breath, waiting for something inevitable but still unknown.

Omar came to stand beside her, his brow furrowed with the same concern that Yasmin felt building inside her. "I don't like this," he muttered, his voice low so the customers wouldn't overhear. "It feels different this time."

Yasmin nodded, her eyes scanning the familiar sights of the street outside—the vendors setting up their stalls, the children running through the alleyways, the mothers gathering at the market. Everything looked the same as it always had, but there was an undercurrent of tension in the air, a sharpness that made her stomach twist. "I know," she admitted softly. "But what can we do?"

Omar didn't respond right away. His eyes were focused on the street, his arms crossed over his chest as if he were trying to shield himself from the invisible threat that hung over them. After a moment, he sighed. "We keep going," he said. "That's all we can do. For now, we keep going."

And so they did. Yasmin threw herself into her work, trying to lose herself in the rhythm of brewing coffee, serving customers, and cleaning up after the morning rush. She tried to ignore the way her hands shook when she heard the faint sound of distant explosions or the way her heart raced when the news came on the radio. She tried to focus on her family—on her father, who had begun to move a little slower as the years wore on; on her younger brothers, who still played in the courtyard as if nothing had changed; on Omar, who had taken to checking the windows more often, his eyes always scanning the horizon as if he could see the future coming toward them.

But the future was not something they could see. It came without warning, like a storm sweeping in from the sea, dark and unrelenting.

It happened on a warm afternoon, a day that had started out much like any other. Yasmin had been in the market, picking up supplies for the shop. The vendors greeted her with smiles and kind words, though she could see the strain behind their eyes, the way their hands moved a little more urgently as they packed up their goods. She could feel it too—that sense that something was coming, that something was about to change.

As she made her way back to the shop, balancing bags of sugar and flour in her arms, the first explosion echoed through the streets.

It was distant but powerful, a deep, reverberating boom that seemed to shake the very ground beneath her feet. Yasmin froze, her heart leaping into her throat as she turned in the direction of the sound. For a moment, the world seemed to stand still. The noise of the market faded away, replaced by the ringing in her ears and the frantic pounding of her heart. She stood there, rooted to the spot, her mind racing with a thousand thoughts, none of them making any sense.

And then, as if on cue, the city erupted into chaos.

People began to scream, their voices rising in panic as another explosion followed the first, this one closer, louder. Vendors abandoned their stalls, grabbing their children and fleeing in every direction. The market, which had been so lively and bustling just moments before, was now a scene of confusion and terror. Yasmin could see the fear in the eyes of the people around her, could hear it in the frantic shouts and cries that filled the air.

She dropped her bags, her instincts taking over as she turned and ran. The coffee shop wasn't far—just a few blocks—but the distance felt like miles as her feet pounded against the pavement. Her heart raced, her breaths coming in short, desperate gasps as she wove through the crowds of people fleeing the market. The explosions continued, each one sending a fresh wave of terror through her. She could feel the ground shake beneath her with each blast, could feel the heat of the fire that had begun to spread through the city.

When she finally reached the coffee shop, Yasmin threw open the door, her chest heaving with exertion. Inside, the atmosphere was tense. The customers had gathered near the windows, their faces pale and fearful as they peered out at the chaos unfolding in the streets.

Omar rushed to her side, his expression one of relief and fear. "Yasmin! Thank God you're safe!"

"I'm fine," Alhamdulillah she gasped, clutching at his arm for support. "What's happening?"

"It's started," Omar said grimly. "The airstrikes... they've begun."

Yasmin's stomach dropped at his words. She had known this was coming—everyone had—but the reality of it still hit her like a blow to the chest. Airstrikes meant destruction. Airstrikes meant death. And there was no telling where the next bomb would fall.

Their father, Abbas, emerged from the back of the shop, his face lined with worry. "We need to close up and get home," he said urgently. "It's not safe here."

Omar nodded, his hand already moving to lock the door. "Everyone, please," he called to the customers. "It's not safe to stay here. Go home, find your families. May Allah protect you all."

The customers didn't need to be told twice. They hurried out of the shop, their faces tight with fear as they made their way into the chaotic streets. Yasmin watched them go, her heart heavy with dread. She knew that some of them might not make it home. She knew that the city she loved was about to be torn apart.

By nightfall, the city had changed. The air was thick with smoke and ash, the once familiar streets now filled with rubble and debris. The sound of explosions had become a constant backdrop to their lives, punctuated by the distant wail of sirens and the frantic shouts of people trying to find safety. Buildings that had once stood tall and proud were now reduced to smouldering ruins, their walls crumbled and broken.

Yasmin sat huddled with her family in the small apartment above the coffee shop. They had closed the shutters and drawn the curtains, trying to block out the horrors unfolding outside, but the sounds still seeped through, an ever-present reminder of the destruction that surrounded them.

Her father sat across from her, his hands clasped tightly together as he muttered prayers under his breath. Beside him, Omar was checking his phone, his brow furrowed in frustration. The internet had been cut off earlier in the day, and now they were cut off from the world, unable to contact the outside or even check on their neighbours.

Hassan and Khaled were curled up on the floor, their faces pale with fear. Khaled clung to his older brother, his small body trembling with each explosion that rocked the city.

"Do you think it will end soon?" Hassan asked quietly, his voice trembling with uncertainty.

Yasmin looked at her younger brothers, her heart breaking for them. They were just children, too young to understand the full scope of what was happening, but old enough to feel the fear that gripped

the city. She wished she could tell them that everything would be okay, that the airstrikes would stop, and that they would wake up to a peaceful morning. But she couldn't lie to them—not now.

"We just have to have faith," she said softly, reaching out to place a hand on Hassan's shoulder. "Allah is with us, even in times like this. We have to trust in Him."

Hassan nodded, though his eyes remained clouded with doubt. He was trying to be brave, trying to hold on to the words of comfort that Yasmin offered, but she could see the fear in his eyes, the uncertainty that had settled over him like a shadow.

The night dragged on, each minute feeling like an eternity. Yasmin sat by the window, her gaze fixed on the darkness outside. Every time an explosion echoed through the streets, her heart skipped a beat, her thoughts immediately turning to the people of Gaza—their friends, their neighbours, the customers who had once filled their coffee shop with laughter and conversation. Were they safe? Had their homes been destroyed? Had their lives been torn apart as completely as hers had been?

It was a question she couldn't answer, and that was perhaps the hardest part of it all. The not knowing. The waiting.

The shadow of war had fallen over Gaza, and Yasmin knew that nothing would ever be the same again.

In the days that followed, the bombings grew more intense, the destruction more widespread. The coffee shop remained closed, the streets too dangerous for anyone to venture out into. Supplies were running low—food, water, medicine—everything was becoming scarce as the siege dragged on.

Yasmin and her family huddled together in the apartment, rationing what little they had left. Each day was a new battle, a struggle for survival in a city that had become a warzone. There were no more quiet mornings, no more bustling markets, no more coffee shop filled with the comforting aroma of freshly brewed coffee. Those days felt like a distant memory, a dream that had slipped away with the coming of the war.

And yet, through it all, Yasmin held on to her faith. She prayed every day, every night, asking Allah for strength, for protection, for peace. It was the only thing she could do, the only thing that gave her hope in the midst of so much darkness.

But even as she prayed, she knew that the worst was still to come. The shadow of war loomed large over their lives, and Yasmin could feel its weight pressing down on her, suffocating her. She knew that this was only the beginning of their struggle, and that more pain, more loss, was waiting just beyond the horizon.

For now, they had each other. For now, they had their faith. But how long would that be enough?

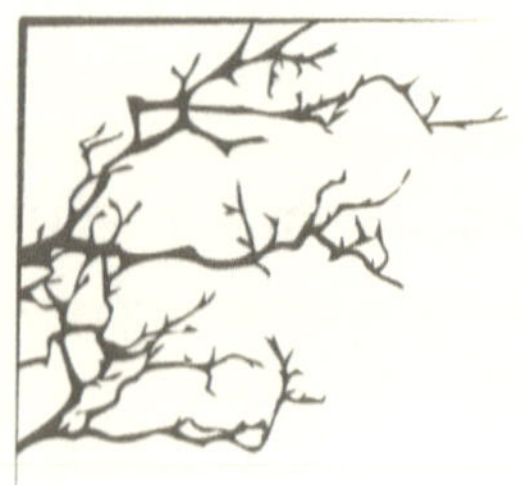

Chapter 2

War Breaks Out

It was a day that would forever be seared into Yasmin's memory, a day that began not with the gentle light of dawn, but with the violent cacophony of war. The night before had been filled with the usual sounds of distant explosions and the rhythmic rumble of airstrikes, but by morning, the violence had intensified. The air was no longer filled with the cries of children playing in the streets or the clatter of vendors setting up stalls, but with the shrill wail of sirens and the roar of fighter jets overhead. Gaza was under siege, and there was no escaping the terror that had gripped the city.

Yasmin woke to the sound of her mother's frantic voice, calling out for everyone to gather in the main room of their small apartment. She scrambled out of bed, her heart pounding in her chest as she rushed to find her younger brothers. Hassan and Khaled were already awake, their faces pale and wide-eyed with fear as they huddled together in the corner of the room. Yasmin pulled them close, wrapping her arms around them in a desperate attempt to offer some semblance of comfort.

Their father, Abbas, was pacing by the window, his face etched with worry as he peered out at the streets below. "It's getting worse," he muttered under his breath, his voice tight with fear. "We need to stay inside, keep the windows covered. No one goes out, understand?"

Yasmin nodded, though the pit of fear in her stomach only seemed to grow with each passing moment. She had never seen her father like this—so visibly shaken, so uncertain. He was the pillar of their family, the one who always knew what to do, no matter how difficult the situation. But now, even he seemed lost in the chaos that had consumed their world.

Omar appeared beside him, his face grim as he loaded supplies into a small bag. "We don't have much left," he said quietly. "We're going to have to ration everything carefully if we're going to make it through this."

Yasmin's heart sank at his words. They had always been a family of modest means, but they had never gone hungry. The coffee shop had provided enough to keep food on the table and a roof over their heads, but now that the shop was closed and the streets were too dangerous to venture out into, their resources were dwindling. The thought of her younger brothers and baby sister going hungry made Yasmin's chest tighten with fear.

Her mother, Ayesha , appeared in the doorway, cradling the new-born baby girl Aaliyah in her arms. "We'll manage," she said softly, her voice calm despite the tension that hung in the air. "We have to. Allah will provide."

Yasmin nodded, though she couldn't shake the feeling of dread that had settled in her chest. She wanted to believe that everything would be okay, that they would survive this, but the fear gnawed at her relentlessly. What if they ran out of food? What if one of the bombs fell on their building? What if the war didn't end?

But there was no time to dwell on those thoughts now. They had to survive, one day at a time.

The first direct hit on their neighbourhood came just after noon.

Yasmin had been in the kitchen, helping her mother prepare what little food they had left for lunch, when the ground shook beneath her feet. The windows rattled violently in their frames, and the sound of the explosion was deafening, a thunderous roar that seemed to echo in her bones. She stumbled backward, her heart racing as the room spun around her.

"Get down!" her mother shouted, grabbing Yasmin by the arm and pulling her to the floor just as another explosion rocked the building. The walls seemed to vibrate with the force of the blast, and Yasmin could hear the sound of glass shattering somewhere nearby.

For a moment, everything was chaos. The air was thick with dust and debris, and the sound of people screaming filled the streets outside. Yasmin pressed her hands to her ears, trying to block out the noise, but it was impossible. The war had come to their doorstep, and there was no escaping it.

After what felt like an eternity, the explosions finally stopped. The ground was still, and the air was eerily quiet. Yasmin slowly lifted her head, blinking through the dust that hung in the air. Her mother was beside her, her face pale and drawn but unharmed. Omar and her father appeared in the doorway, their faces grim but relieved to see that everyone was safe.

"Are you alright?" her father asked, his voice tight with worry as he helped Yasmin and her mother to their feet.

Yasmin nodded shakily, though her heart was still racing in her chest. "I'm fine," she whispered, though her voice was barely audible over the ringing in her ears. She glanced around the room, taking in the damage. The windows had been blown out, and shards of glass littered the floor. The walls were cracked, and a thick layer of dust covered everything.

Hassan and Khaled appeared in the doorway, their faces pale and frightened. "Is it over?" Hassan asked quietly, his voice trembling with fear.

Omar knelt down beside them, pulling them into a tight hug. "For now," he said softly. "But we need to stay vigilant. We don't know when the next strike will come."

Yasmin's stomach churned at his words. The reality of their situation was beginning to sink in. This wasn't just a temporary danger. The war was here to stay, and they would have to endure it for as long as it lasted.

In the days that followed, the airstrikes became more frequent, the bombings more intense. Every few hours, the ground would shake with the force of the explosions, and the sky would light up with the flash of missiles and gunfire. The once vibrant streets of Gaza were now filled with rubble and debris, the air thick with smoke and ash. Buildings that had once stood tall and proud were now reduced to crumbling ruins, their walls blackened by fire and their windows shattered.

Yasmin and her family remained huddled together in their apartment, venturing out only when absolutely necessary. The streets were too dangerous, filled with falling debris and the constant threat of airstrikes. Food was becoming scarce, and the sound of crying children echoed through the building as families struggled to survive.

One afternoon, Omar and Yasmin made the decision to brave the streets and search for supplies. They knew it was a risk, but they had no choice. Their food stores were nearly depleted, and their baby sister needed formula, something they hadn't been able to find in days.

"Stay together," their father warned as they prepared to leave. "And if you hear the sirens, get inside immediately. No hesitation."

Yasmin nodded, her heart pounding with fear as she followed Omar out the door. The streets were eerily quiet, the once bustling market now deserted. The buildings around them were in various states of collapse, their windows blown out and their walls crumbling. The smell of smoke and burning debris hung heavy in the air, and Yasmin could feel the weight of the war pressing down on her with every step.

They moved quickly, their eyes scanning the streets for any sign of danger. Yasmin's heart raced with every sound, every distant explosion, her mind constantly calculating the distance between them and the nearest shelter. She kept close to Omar, her hands trembling as she clutched the empty shopping bag in her grip.

When they finally reached the market, Yasmin felt a brief flicker of relief. Some of the vendors had returned, setting up makeshift stalls amidst the ruins of their former shops. The selection was sparse—mostly canned goods and stale bread—but it was something.

Yasmin moved from stall to stall, gathering what little she could find: a bag of rice, a few cans of beans, and a small loaf of bread. She glanced at Omar, who was searching for baby formula, his brow furrowed with worry as he rummaged through the scattered supplies.

"Anything?" Yasmin asked, her voice tight with concern.

Omar shook his head, his expression grim. "Nothing. We might have to try another market."

Yasmin's heart sank at his words. She knew that moving through the streets was dangerous, especially with the airstrikes becoming more frequent. But they had no choice. Their baby sister was starving, and they couldn't go back empty-handed.

"Let's try the next street," she suggested, her voice shaky but determined. "We can't give up yet."

Omar nodded, and they moved on, their footsteps echoing through the empty streets. The tension in the air was palpable, every sound making Yasmin jump as they made their way to the next market. She could feel the weight of the war pressing down on her, the fear gnawing at her insides with every step.

They had only just reached the next market when the sirens began to wail.

Yasmin's heart leaped into her throat as she froze, her mind racing with panic. The airstrike warnings had become all too familiar, but that didn't make them any less terrifying. She glanced at Omar, her eyes wide with fear as she looked for shelter.

"There!" Omar shouted, pointing to a nearby building that had somehow survived the bombings. It was little more than a shell, its windows shattered and its walls cracked, but it offered some protection from the incoming missiles.

They ran, their footsteps pounding against the pavement as the sound of explosions grew louder in the distance. Yasmin's heart raced, her breath coming in short, frantic gasps as they sprinted toward the building. She could feel the heat of the explosions behind her , the ground shaking beneath her feet as the missiles struck the city.

When they finally reached the building, they threw themselves inside, their bodies trembling with fear and exhaustion. Yasmin pressed her back against the wall, her chest heaving as she tried to catch her breath. Omar was beside her, his face pale and drawn as he peered out the shattered window.

The city was in flames.

Yasmin's heart sank as she looked out at the devastation that surrounded them. Buildings were crumbling, their walls collapsing under the force of the airstrikes. The streets were filled with debris, and the air was thick with smoke and ash. The once familiar sights of Gaza were now nothing more than a warzone, a place where death and destruction reigned supreme.

"We have to get back," Omar said quietly, his voice tight with fear. "It's not safe out here."

Yasmin nodded, though her legs felt like lead as she pushed herself to her feet. The world around her felt surreal, like a nightmare she couldn't wake up from. Every step she took felt like a step further into the abyss, a place where hope and safety no longer existed.

By the time they returned to the apartment, Yasmin was numb. The day had taken its toll on her, physically and emotionally. She collapsed onto the floor, her body trembling with exhaustion as she dropped the bags of supplies beside her. Omar sat beside her, his face etched with the same weariness that she felt deep in her bones.

Their father appeared in the doorway, his eyes filled with relief as he saw them both alive and safe. Alhamdulillah "Thank Allah you're back," he said quietly, his voice filled with emotion. "We were so worried."

Yasmin managed a weak smile, though it didn't reach her eyes. "We got what we could," she said softly, her voice barely above a whisper. "But it's not much."

Her father nodded, his expression sober as he knelt beside her. "It's enough for now," he said gently. "You did well. Both of you."

Yasmin closed her eyes, letting out a shaky breath as she leaned back against the wall. She could feel the weight of the day pressing down on her, the exhaustion seeping into her bones. But even in the midst of her weariness, she couldn't shake the feeling of dread that gnawed at her insides.

The war was far from over, and they were only at the beginning of their struggle. Every day would be a battle for survival, every moment a test of their strength and resilience. And Yasmin knew that the worst was still to come.

But for now, they had made it through another day. And in Gaza, that was all that mattered.

The days blurred together in a haze of fear and exhaustion. The bombings continued, each strike sending shockwaves through the city and leaving more destruction in its wake. Yasmin and her family huddled together in their apartment, venturing out only when absolutely necessary. Food was scarce, and the sound of crying children echoed through the building as families struggled to survive.

One night, the explosions were louder than ever before. Yasmin woke to the sound of glass shattering and the building shaking violently beneath her. She scrambled out of bed, her heart racing with fear as she rushed to check on her family. Her father was already at the window, his face pale as he peered out into the darkness.

"It's close," he whispered, his voice tight with fear. "Too close."

Yasmin's stomach churned with dread as she looked out the window. The sky was lit up with the orange glow of fire, and the sound of distant screams filled the air. The bombings had intensified, and it was clear that the war was closing in on them.

"We need to get out of here," Omar said quietly, his voice steady but filled with urgency. "We can't stay here any longer. It's too dangerous."

Yasmin's heart sank at his words. The thought of leaving their home, their city, was almost too much to bear. But deep down, she knew he was right. The war had consumed Gaza, and staying in the city would only put them in more danger.

Their father nodded, his expression grim as he turned away from the window. "We'll leave in the morning," he said quietly. "Pack only what we need. We'll head for the refugee camp in Rafah."

Yasmin's heart clenched at the thought of the refugee camp. She had heard stories of the conditions there—stories of overcrowding, disease, and starvation. But it was the only option they had left. The war had taken everything from them, and now all they could do was try to survive.

As the first light of dawn broke over the horizon, Yasmin and her family gathered what little they had left and prepared to leave their home. The city was eerily quiet, the usual sounds of life replaced by the distant rumble of explosions and the crackle of fire. The streets were empty, save for the occasional figure darting between the shadows, their faces etched with fear.

Yasmin's heart ached as she looked around the city she had grown up in, the city that had once been filled with life and laughter. Now, it was nothing more than a warzone, a place where death and destruction reigned supreme. She felt a lump form in her throat as she looked at the crumbling buildings, the shattered windows, and the streets filled with debris.

This wasn't the Gaza she had known. This was a place torn apart by war, a place where hope had been replaced by fear and despair.

With a heavy heart, Yasmin turned away from the city and followed her family into the unknown. The road ahead would be difficult, filled with danger and uncertainty, but they had no choice. They had to leave. They had to survive.

And so, with one last glance at the city she loved, Yasmin stepped into the future—into a world where war had shattered everything she had once known, and where survival was the only thing that mattered.

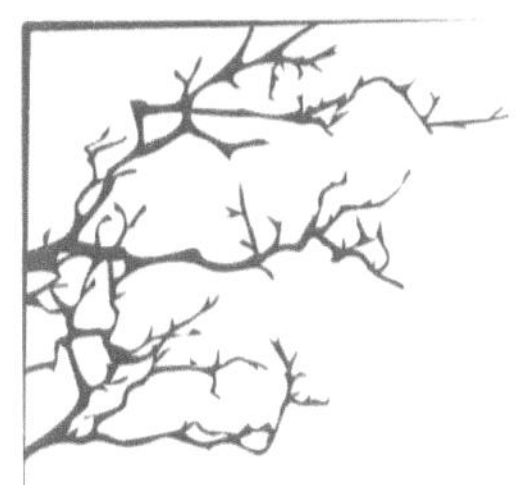

Chapter 3

The Siege of Starvation

The journey to Khan Younis was fraught with danger from the start. Yasmin, Omar, their mother Ayesha , and her two younger brothers—Hassan and Khaled had left behind the ruins of Gaza City under the cover of darkness, their footsteps muted by the thick layer of dust and debris that blanketed the once-bustling streets. They carried only the essentials: a small bag of food, what little water they had, and the clothing on their backs. With each step, the echoes of war followed them distant explosions, the hum of drones overhead, and the ever-present crackle of gunfire.

Khan Younis was supposed to be a safer place, a city far enough from the heaviest fighting that perhaps they could find refuge. But as they neared the outskirts of the city, it became painfully clear that no place in Gaza was safe. The war had spread like a disease, infecting every corner of the land, leaving no sanctuary untouched.

The roads were perilous, crisscrossed with makeshift checkpoints, debris, and craters from past airstrikes. The family moved silently, keeping close to the shadows and avoiding the open streets as much as possible. Omar took the lead, his eyes constantly scanning the area for any sign of danger, while Abbas, their father, walked beside Yasmin, keeping a protective hand on her shoulder.

They had been walking for hours when the first crack of gunfire split the air. It was a sharp, sudden sound, like the snap of a whip, and it made Yasmin's heart leap into her throat. She dropped to the ground instinctively, pulling Hassan and Khaled down with her, her breath coming in shallow, panicked gasps.

"Snipers," Omar hissed, his voice barely audible over the ringing in Yasmin's ears. "Stay low."

Yasmin's heart raced as she pressed herself against the ground, the rough gravel digging into her palms. She could feel Hassan trembling beside her, his small hands clutching at her shirt as he tried to control his fear. Khaled, too young to fully understand the danger, was eerily quiet, his wide eyes filled with confusion.

Her father, Abbas, was already on his feet, his eyes scanning the surrounding buildings for any sign of the sniper's position. "We need to move," he said urgently, his voice low but commanding. "Stay close to the walls, and keep your heads down."

Before they could move, another sound pierced the air—this time, it wasn't the crack of a sniper rifle, but the high-pitched cry of a child.

Yasmin's blood ran cold as she turned her head, searching for the source of the sound. There, just a few meters away, was a small boy, no older than seven or eight, crouching in the middle of the street. He was alone, his eyes wide with terror as he clutched a tattered blanket to his chest. His body shook with sobs, his face streaked with dirt and tears.

"No," Yasmin whispered, her heart breaking at the sight of the boy. "He's just a child."

Her father's face tightened with grim determination as he locked eyes with Yasmin. She knew what he was thinking even before he spoke.

"Stay here," Abbas ordered, his voice low and firm. "Don't move."

"No, Baba!" Yasmin reached out, grabbing his arm, her eyes pleading with him. "You can't. It's too dangerous."

But Abbas had already made up his mind. He gently pried her fingers from his arm, giving her a small, sad smile. "I can't leave him there," he said softly. "I won't."

Before Yasmin could protest further, her father was on his feet, moving swiftly toward the boy. The street was wide and exposed, offering little in the way of cover, but Abbas moved with a quiet, calculated grace, keeping low and staying close to the shadows as he approached the child.

Yasmin's heart pounded in her chest as she watched her father move. Her breath caught in her throat, her fingers digging into the dirt beneath her as she prayed silently for his safety. "Please, Allah, protect him," she whispered, her voice trembling with fear.

Abbas reached the boy in a matter of seconds, though it felt like hours to Yasmin. He knelt down beside the child, speaking to him in soft, soothing tones. The boy looked up at him, his tear-streaked face filled with confusion and fear, but Abbas reached out, gently placing a hand on the boy's shoulder as he coaxed him to his feet.

For a moment, it seemed as though they would make it.

Then came the shot.

Yasmin didn't see where it came from—she didn't have time. All she heard was the sickening crack of the rifle, followed by the sound of her father's body hitting the ground.

"No!" Yasmin screamed, her voice raw with anguish as she scrambled to her feet. Her legs felt like lead, her body numb with shock, but she ran toward her father, her heart pounding in her ears as the world seemed to blur around her.

She reached him just as the boy collapsed beside him, both of them lying motionless in the dirt, their blood pooling beneath them. Yasmin dropped to her knees, her hands shaking as she reached out to touch her father's face, her fingers trembling as they brushed against his still-warm skin.

"Baba, please," she whispered, her voice breaking as tears streamed down her face. "Please don't leave us."

But Abbas didn't respond. His eyes were closed, his chest still, and Yasmin knew in that moment that he was gone.

There was no time to grieve.

The sniper was still out there, and they were still in danger. Omar appeared beside her, his face pale and drawn with shock, but his eyes were focused and determined. He grabbed Yasmin by the arm, pulling her to her feet.

"We have to go," he said urgently, his voice tight with emotion. "Now."

Yasmin wanted to scream, wanted to fall to the ground and weep for her father, but she knew Omar was right. They couldn't stay here. Not with the sniper still watching. Not with Hassan and Khaled waiting for her to come back.

She forced herself to move, her body shaking with adrenaline and grief as she followed Omar back to where her brothers and mother were waiting. Her heart felt like it was being torn from her chest, but there was no time to dwell on the pain. They had to survive. They had to keep moving.

Her mother's face was ashen, her eyes wide with shock as she saw Yasmin and Omar returning without Abbas. She didn't need to ask what had happened—she knew. The grief in her eyes was too deep for words, and Yasmin felt her heart break all over again as she met her mother's gaze.

But there was no time to cry. No time to mourn.

"Keep your heads down," Omar said urgently, his voice a low whisper as he ushered them toward the next street. "We need to get out of here before the sniper locks onto us again."

Yasmin moved mechanically, her mind numb as they weaved through the narrow alleys and side streets of Khan Younis. The world around her felt surreal, like a nightmare she couldn't wake up from. Every step felt heavier than the last, her legs trembling with exhaustion and grief.

But there was no stopping. No resting. They had to keep going.

As the sun began to set, casting long shadows over the ruined streets, they finally reached a safer area—a small, bombed-out building that offered some semblance of shelter from the dangers outside. They collapsed inside, their bodies trembling with exhaustion as they huddled together in the dark.

Yasmin felt the weight of the day pressing down on her, the loss of her father crushing her chest with every breath. She wanted to cry, to scream, to mourn the man who had given his life to save a child. But the grief was too heavy, too overwhelming. She couldn't let herself fall apart—not yet.

Her mother sat in the corner, her face pale and gaunt as she cradled Khaled in her arms. Hassan sat beside her, his eyes wide and vacant as he stared at the wall. No one spoke. The silence was suffocating, broken only by the distant sounds of war that echoed through the city.

Omar was the first to speak. His voice was low, steady, but filled with a quiet grief that mirrored Yasmin's own. "We'll keep moving in the morning," he said softly, his eyes fixed on the ground. "We'll head for the camp in Rafah. It's the only safe place left."

Yasmin nodded numbly, though she wasn't sure if anywhere in Gaza could truly be called safe. But what choice did they have? They couldn't stay here. Not with the snipers, the bombings, the starvation. They had to keep moving. They had to survive.

But as Yasmin sat there, her body trembling with exhaustion and grief, she couldn't shake the feeling that the worst was still to come. They had already lost so much, endured so much. But the war was far from over, and Yasmin knew that the path ahead would be even harder than the one they had already walked.

She closed her eyes, her heart heavy with sorrow as she whispered a silent prayer.

"Please, Allah," she whispered, her voice barely audible in the darkness. "Give us strength. Protect us. Help us survive."

And in the stillness of the night, as the war raged on outside, Yasmin clung to that prayer like a lifeline, hoping

against hope that they would make it through another day.

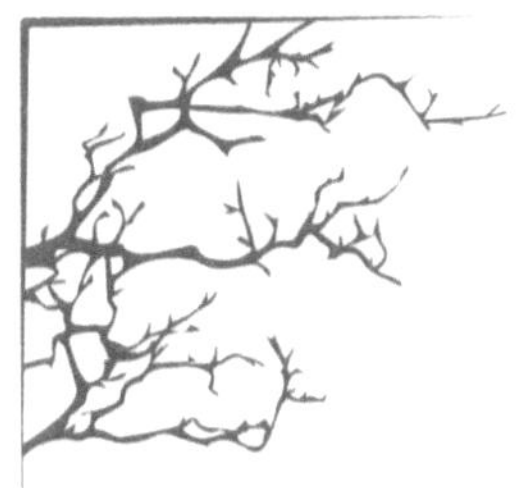

Chapter 4

Fleeing to Rafah

The dawn brought no respite from the violence, only the reality of what they had lost. Yasmin sat in the corner of the bombed-out building, her body trembling with exhaustion. The air was thick with dust, the smell of smoke and gunpowder still lingering from the battle that had raged the night before. Her mind was numb, and her heart ached with a grief too profound to express. She glanced at her mother, Ayesha , who sat silently beside her, cradling Khaled and Aaliyah new born baby in her arms. Omar leaned against the cracked wall, his face pale, dark circles under his eyes. Hassan sat beside him, eyes wide and vacant.

There had been no time to mourn Abbas's death. The moment they had pulled Yasmin away from his body, their sole focus had been on survival. The image of her father lying still in the street, shot down as he tried to save a child, haunted her mind. Every time Yasmin closed her eyes, she saw him, his stillness, the blood pooling around him. She wanted to scream, to cry, to let the flood of emotions out, but nothing came. She was hollow, empty inside.

Omar cleared his throat, breaking the suffocating silence. His voice was hoarse, barely above a whisper. "We need to move. We can't stay here."

Yasmin looked up at him, her throat tight. She knew he was right. The small shelter they had found was nothing more than a temporary reprieve. The sniper that had taken their father could still be out there, waiting for their next move. They had to keep going, had to get to Rafah, the refuge camp where they hoped to find safety.

"We'll leave at first light," Omar continued, his gaze fixed on the floor. "We should be able to make it to Rafah by nightfall if we keep moving."

Yasmin nodded numbly. The thought of walking all the way to Rafah with so little food and water was daunting, but there was no other option. They couldn't stay here, exposed and vulnerable. The camp was their only hope, no matter how difficult the journey might be.

Her mother's voice was soft, barely audible. "How much food do we have left?"

Omar sighed, running a hand through his hair. "Not much. Just the rice and a few cans of beans we found. Water is even worse—we're almost out."

Yasmin's stomach twisted at his words. The hunger that had gnawed at her for days was now a constant ache, and the thought of running out of water made her throat feel even drier. But they had no choice. They would have to ration what little they had and pray that they made it to Rafah before it ran out.

They spent the rest of the morning gathering what few supplies they had. Yasmin helped her mother pack the small bag they had brought from their home, tucking the cans of beans and the rice into the bottom. There was barely enough food to last them a day, and Yasmin couldn't help but wonder if they would survive the journey at all.

As the sun rose higher in the sky, casting long shadows across the ruined streets, they prepared to leave. Yasmin took one last look at the shelter that had provided them with a brief moment of safety, then turned to face the road ahead. Omar led the way, his eyes scanning the area for any sign of danger, while Yasmin walked beside her mother, her mother was carrying the baby girl Aaliyah , one hand resting protectively on Khaled's shoulder.

The road to Rafah was long and perilous, stretching across the war-torn landscape of southern Gaza. Every step they took was accompanied by the distant rumble of explosions, the faint echo of gunfire. The air was thick with tension, the ever-present threat of snipers and bombings hanging over them like a shroud.

They moved as quickly as they could, sticking to the side streets and narrow alleyways, avoiding the open roads where they might be seen. The city was a ghost town, its streets littered with debris and rubble, the remnants of homes and businesses that had been reduced to ruins by the relentless bombings. The silence was eerie, broken only by the occasional cry of a bird or the distant wail of a siren.

By midday, the sun was high in the sky, beating down on them with unrelenting heat. Yasmin's throat was parched, her lips cracked and dry, and every step felt like a struggle. Khaled had begun to slow, his small legs struggling to keep up with the pace. Yasmin could see the exhaustion in his eyes, the way his little body trembled with each step, but there was nothing she could do to ease his suffering. They had to keep moving.

"Let's stop for a moment," Omar said, his voice tight with strain. He gestured toward a small, shaded alleyway, where they could rest for a few minutes and catch their breath.

Yasmin gratefully sank down onto the cool stone, her legs trembling with exhaustion. She pulled Khaled close, wrapping her arm around his small frame as he leaned against her, his head resting on her shoulder. Hassan sat down beside them, his face pale and drawn with fatigue.

"We don't have much further to go," Omar said, though Yasmin could hear the doubt in his voice. They were still miles from Rafah, and the sun was already beginning to sink lower in the sky. If they didn't reach the camp by nightfall, they would have to spend the night exposed in the open.

"Are you sure we'll make it before dark?" Yasmin asked quietly, her voice trembling with fear.

Omar's jaw tightened, and he glanced away, unable to meet her gaze. "We'll do our best," he said finally. "But we have to keep moving. We can't stop for long."

Yasmin nodded, though her heart sank at his words. She could feel the weight of their situation pressing down on her, the fear and uncertainty gnawing at her insides. But she knew Omar was right. They had no choice but to keep going.

After a few minutes of rest, they gathered their things and set off again. The streets were eerily quiet, the once-bustling city now reduced to a wasteland of crumbling buildings and shattered glass. Yasmin kept her head down, her eyes focused on the ground as they walked, trying to block out the images of destruction that surrounded them.

As the afternoon wore on, the hunger in Yasmin's belly became unbearable. They hadn't eaten anything since the day before, and the gnawing emptiness was making her feel weak, her legs trembling with every step. She knew the rest of her family was suffering just as much, but there was nothing they could do. The little food they had left needed to be rationed, and they couldn't afford to stop long enough to prepare it.

Omar glanced back at them, his brow furrowed with worry. "We'll eat when we reach the next safe spot," he promised, though Yasmin could hear the uncertainty in his voice. Safe spots were few and far between, and they hadn't found one yet.

"Just a little longer," Yasmin whispered to herself, her voice barely audible over the sound of their footsteps. She didn't know if she was trying to convince herself or Khaled, who was stumbling along beside her, his face pale and gaunt from hunger.

Finally, as the sun dipped low on the horizon, they came across a small building that appeared to be intact. Omar motioned for them to stop, his eyes scanning the area for any signs of danger before he led them inside.

The building was empty, its walls cracked and blackened from past bombings, but it provided some shelter from the dangers outside. They settled down in the corner of the room, their bodies trembling with exhaustion.

Yasmin pulled the small bag of food from her pack and handed it to her mother, who quickly divided the meagre rations among them. It wasn't much—just a small portion of rice and beans—but it was better than nothing. Yasmin ate slowly, savouring each bite, though the food did little to ease the hunger that gnawed at her insides.

As they ate, Omar kept a watchful eye on the door, his body tense with worry. "We'll rest here for the night," he said quietly. "But we need to leave at first light. If we're lucky, we'll reach Rafah by midday."

Yasmin nodded, though her heart was heavy with doubt. The road ahead was still long, and they were all growing weaker with each passing day. But she knew they had no choice. They had to keep going.

The night was restless, filled with the sounds of distant explosions and the constant hum of drones overhead. Yasmin lay awake, her mind racing with fear and uncertainty. She could hear her mother's soft prayers in the corner, the whispered words of faith that were the only thing keeping them going.

"Please, Allah, keep us safe," Yasmin whispered, her voice trembling as tears filled her eyes. She didn't know how much more they could endure. They had already lost so much—her father, their home, their safety. But the thought of losing her brothers, her mother, was too much to bear.

Eventually, exhaustion overtook her, and she fell into a fitful sleep.

By morning, they were on the move again, their bodies aching with fatigue as they set off toward Rafah. The air was cooler in the early hours, but the weight of the sun was already beginning to press down on them as it rose higher in the sky.

The closer they got to Rafah, the more dangerous the roads became. They passed through small villages that had been reduced to rubble, the remains

of homes and shops scattered across the streets. The smell of death lingered in the air, and Yasmin had to cover her nose with her sleeve to block out the stench.

"We're close," Omar said, his voice tight with tension. "But we need to be careful. The camp is just beyond that ridge, but there's been fighting in the area. We'll have to move quickly."

Yasmin's heart pounded in her chest as she followed Omar's lead, her eyes scanning the horizon for any sign of danger. The thought of finally reaching the camp filled her with both hope and fear. Would they find safety there? Or would they find more of the same destruction that had followed them all the way from Gaza?

As they neared the ridge, the sound of gunfire echoed through the air, and Yasmin's stomach twisted with fear. Omar motioned for them to crouch low, his body tense as he scanned the area for the source of the gunfire.

"We have to go now," he whispered urgently, his voice barely audible over the sound of the fighting. "Stay low and follow me. Don't stop for anything."

Yasmin nodded, her heart racing as she grabbed Khaled's hand and pulled him close. Her mother and Hassan were right behind them, their faces pale with fear as they crouched low and followed Omar over the ridge.

The camp was in sight, just a few hundred meters away, but the ground between them and safety was a battlefield. Yasmin could see the flash of gunfire in the distance, the figures of soldiers moving through the streets. Her heart pounded in her chest as they moved quickly, their bodies pressed low to the ground as they sprinted toward the camp.

Suddenly, a loud explosion ripped through the air, and Yasmin was thrown to the ground by the force of the blast. She gasped for breath, her ears ringing as she struggled to push herself up. Her vision was blurry, and for a moment, she couldn't hear anything but the dull roar of the explosion.

"Yasmin!" Omar's voice cut through the haze, and she felt his hands on her shoulders, pulling her to her feet. "We have to go! Now!"

Yasmin nodded, her legs trembling as she stumbled forward, her mind reeling from the shock of the explosion. She could hear Khaled crying beside her, his small hand gripping hers tightly as they moved as quickly as they could toward the camp.

They had almost reached the gates when another explosion rocked the ground beneath them, and Yasmin felt a sharp pain in her side. She stumbled, gasping for breath as she pressed a hand to her ribs, feeling the warm, sticky wetness of blood beneath her fingers.

But there was no time to stop. No time to think about the pain. They had to keep moving.

Omar grabbed her arm, pulling her forward as they finally reached the gates of the camp. The soldiers at the entrance waved them through, their faces grim as they ushered them inside.

Yasmin collapsed onto the ground just beyond the gates, her body trembling with exhaustion and pain. The world around her seemed to spin, and she could feel the darkness closing in at the edges of her vision.

But as she lay there, gasping for breath, she felt a glimmer of hope. They had made it.

They were safe just for now.

The camp was nothing like Yasmin had imagined. Instead of a place of refuge and safety, it was a sprawling mass of tents and makeshift shelters, overcrowded with families who had fled the violence just as they had. The air was thick with the smell of unwashed bodies and the acrid scent of burning garbage, and the sounds of crying children and the murmurs of worried parents filled the air.

Yasmin's side throbbed with pain, but she forced herself to stand, leaning heavily on Omar as they made their way through the camp. They were directed to a small tent near the edge of the camp, where a few blankets had been laid out on the ground.

"It's not much," one of the aid workers said, her voice tired and weary. "But it's all we have right now."

Yasmin nodded gratefully, though her heart sank as she looked around at the cramped, dirty space. It was a far cry from the home they had once had, but at least they were together. At least they were alive.

As they settled into the tent, Yasmin's mother knelt beside her, gently pulling back the fabric of her shirt to inspect the wound on her side. "It's not too deep," she said softly, her voice trembling with worry. "But we need to clean it, or it could get infected."

Omar handed her a small bottle of water, and Yasmin's mother carefully cleaned the wound as best she could. The pain was sharp and searing, but Yasmin gritted her teeth, refusing to cry out.

"We'll rest here for a few days," Omar said quietly, his voice filled with exhaustion. "But we need to be careful. The camp is overcrowded, and food and water are scarce. We'll have to be smart about how we ration what we have."

Yasmin nodded, though her mind was still reeling from the events of the past few days. They had made it to the camp, but the reality of their situation was still sinking in. They were safe from the immediate danger of the bombings and snipers, but now they faced a new set of challenges—starvation, disease, and the constant uncertainty of life in the camp.

But for now, all Yasmin could do was rest. She lay back on the blanket, her body trembling with exhaustion, and closed her eyes.

And for the first time in days, she allowed herself to cry.

The days that followed blurred together in a haze of exhaustion and hunger. The camp was overcrowded, and the aid trucks that arrived sporadically were barely enough to feed everyone. They were given small rations of rice and water, but it was never enough. Yasmin's stomach ached with hunger, and her body grew weaker with each passing day.

Omar had taken it upon himself to help around the camp, doing whatever he could to assist the aid workers in distributing food and water. He spent long hours standing in line for their rations, and Yasmin could see the toll it was taking on him. His face was gaunt, his eyes sunken with fatigue, but he refused to rest.

"We have to do what we can to survive," he said quietly one night, as they sat huddled together in their small tent. "We can't just sit here and wait for things to get worse."

Yasmin nodded, though her heart was heavy with doubt. She could see the strain in her mother's face, the way her hands trembled as she tried to comfort Khaled and Hassan. They were all growing weaker, specially the baby it was malnutrition and the fear of what might happen if the aid trucks stopped coming was always at the back of their minds.

But there was nothing they could do except wait.

One morning, as Yasmin was helping her mother clean the tent, Omar appeared at the entrance, his face pale and drawn.

"The aid trucks are here," he said quietly. "I'm going to try to get us more food."

Yasmin's heart leaped at his words. They had barely eaten the day before, and the thought of more food was almost too good to be true. But as she looked at Omar, she could see the exhaustion in his eyes, the way his body trembled with fatigue.

"I'll come with you," she said, her voice steady despite the fear that gnawed at her insides.

Omar shook his head. "No. Stay here with Mama and the boys. I'll be back soon."

Yasmin wanted to argue, but she knew there was no point. Omar had always been the protector, the one who took on the burden of their survival. She watched as he disappeared into the crowd, her heart heavy with worry.

The hours passed slowly, and as the sun began to set, Yasmin's worry grew. Omar hadn't returned, and the camp was growing restless. The sounds of arguing and shouting filled the air as people fought over the dwindling rations, and Yasmin's stomach twisted with fear.

She stood at the entrance of their tent, her eyes scanning the crowded camp for any sign of Omar. But as the minutes ticked by, her hope began to fade.

And then she saw him.

Omar was running, his face pale with fear as he sprinted toward their tent. Yasmin's heart leaped into her throat as she rushed toward him, her legs trembling with exhaustion.

"Omar!" she called, her voice trembling. "What happened?"

But before Omar could answer, the sound of gunfire echoed through the camp, and Yasmin's blood ran cold.

The soldiers had arrived.

They had come to take the aid, to steal what little food and water was left. Chaos erupted in the camp as people scattered, their screams filling the air as they tried to flee the violence.

Omar grabbed Yasmin's arm, pulling her toward their tent. "We have to go," he said urgently. "Now."

Yasmin's heart pounded in her chest as they rushed back to their tent, grabbing their mother and brothers. They had no time to gather their things, no time to think about anything except survival.

The camp was in chaos as they fled, the sounds of gunfire and explosions filling the air. Yasmin could feel her legs trembling with exhaustion, her breath coming in short, frantic gasps as they ran.

But there was no stopping. No turning back.

They had to keep moving.

By the time they reached the outskirts of the camp, Yasmin's body was trembling with exhaustion. They had managed to escape the violence, but the fear still gnawed at her insides.

"We can't stay here," Omar said quietly, his voice tight with strain. "We'll have to keep moving, find somewhere else to go."

Yasmin nodded, though her heart was heavy with uncertainty. They had escaped the camp, but now they were once again on the run, with no food, no water, and no idea where to go.

But they had no choice.

They had to keep going.

They had to survive.

The days that followed were a blur of exhaustion and hunger. They moved from place to place, never staying in one spot for too long, always on the lookout for danger. The war had consumed every part of Gaza, and finding food and water was becoming increasingly difficult.

Yasmin's body grew weaker with each passing day, her legs trembling with fatigue as they walked. The hunger was a constant ache in her belly, and her throat was so dry that it hurt to swallow. She could see the same weakness in her brothers and her mother, and it broke her heart.

But there was nothing they could do except keep moving.

One night, as they huddled together under a makeshift shelter, Omar spoke quietly, his voice barely audible over the sound of the wind.

"We can't keep doing this," he said, his voice trembling with exhaustion. "We need to find a place where we can stay, where we can rest."

Yasmin nodded, though her heart was heavy with doubt. Finding a place to rest seemed impossible. The war had consumed everything, and the thought of finding a safe place to stay felt like a distant dream.

But they had no choice.

They had to keep going.
They had to survive.

41

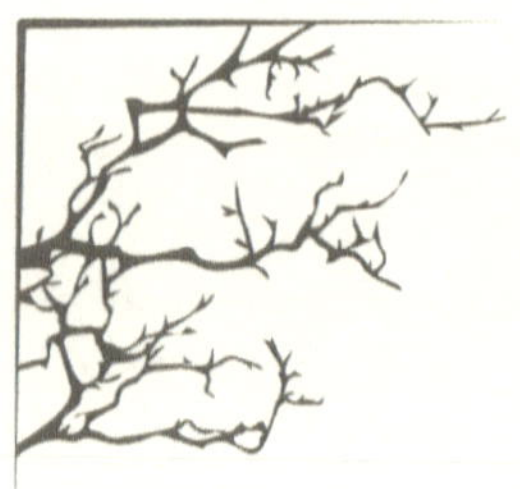

Chapter 5

The Loss of Another

The days passed like a blur, each one blending into the next as Yasmin's family moved through the war-torn landscape, their bodies and spirits weighed down by the unrelenting hunger, exhaustion, and fear that had become their constant companions. Every step they took seemed to drag them deeper into despair, the path ahead more uncertain with each passing hour. The war had consumed everything, leaving only the hollow shell of the world they once knew.

Omar led them through the desolate streets, his face grim and determined, though Yasmin could see the toll the journey was taking on him. He had always been their protector, their rock, but even he was beginning to crack under the weight of it all. His eyes were dark with fatigue, his once strong and steady hands now trembling with exhaustion. Yet, he never complained, never let his own suffering show. He carried the burden of their survival silently, as though it was his duty alone to keep them safe.

Yasmin, too, felt the crushing weight of their circumstances. Her body had grown weak from starvation, her legs trembling with every step, her vision often blurring as dizziness overtook her. But she forced herself to keep going, driven by the need to protect her younger brothers, Hassan and Khaled, and her mother, Ayesha , who had grown more frail with each passing day. The hunger gnawed at her insides, an ever-present reminder of their dwindling supplies. They hadn't eaten in days, and what little water they had left was carefully rationed, each sip a precious commodity.

BENEATH THE ASHES A TESTAMENT OF FAITH

The road to survival was long and cruel, and Yasmin knew that not all of them would make it. The fear of losing another family member clung to her like a shadow, always there, lurking just beyond the edge of her consciousness. They had already lost so much—her father, their home, their way of life. But the war was far from over, and Yasmin knew the worst was still to come.

They had been walking for days, the landscape around them growing more desolate with each passing mile. The streets were littered with debris and the remnants of lives torn apart by the war. Shattered windows, crumbling buildings, and the skeletal remains of cars lined their path, a stark reminder of the destruction that had ravaged Gaza. The smell of smoke and burning wood lingered in the air, a constant companion to the distant sounds of gunfire and explosions that echoed across the horizon.

They moved cautiously, sticking to the shadows and avoiding the main roads where they might be spotted by soldiers or snipers. Every step was taken with the knowledge that danger could be lurking around any corner, and the fear of being caught or shot weighed heavily on them all. Even the children, Khaled and Hassan, had grown silent, their once lively spirits dampened by the horrors they had witnessed.

Omar stopped suddenly, raising a hand to signal for the others to halt. Yasmin's heart skipped a beat as she followed his gaze, her eyes scanning the road ahead. There was movement in the distance—shadows darting between the buildings, too far away to make out clearly but close enough to send a wave of fear through her.

"Soldiers?" she whispered, her voice barely audible.

Omar shook his head, his brow furrowed with concentration. "I don't think so. Could be other refugees, or..." He trailed off, not wanting to voice the possibility of looters or bandits. In times like these, not everyone was driven by survival alone. Desperation could turn even the most honourable people into something far more dangerous.

"We'll go around," Omar decided, his voice steady despite the tension in his posture. "Stick close and stay quiet."

Yasmin nodded, clutching Khaled's hand tightly as they turned and moved toward a narrow alleyway that wound its way between the buildings. The walls loomed high on either side, casting long shadows that made the space feel claustrophobic. Every sound seemed amplified in the narrow passage—the scuff of their feet against the dirt, the ragged breaths of her family as they fought to keep moving.

The sun was beginning to set, casting the sky in shades of deep orange and crimson, the light filtering through the haze of smoke that hung over the city. Yasmin's legs ached with every step, the exhaustion creeping into her bones, but she pushed on, driven by the thought of finding safety, of finally being able to rest. Yet, even as she clung to that hope, she knew in her heart that safety was a fleeting concept in Gaza. There was no refuge from the war, only brief moments of respite before the next wave of violence crashed down upon them.

They emerged from the alley into a small courtyard, the space eerily quiet and still. Yasmin glanced around, her heart pounding in her chest as she scanned the area for any signs of danger. The buildings here were crumbling, their facades blackened by fire and neglect. Windows gaped open like hollow eyes, and the street was littered with debris—broken furniture, shards of glass, and the remnants of lives long abandoned.

Omar motioned for them to take cover behind a half-collapsed wall, and they crouched low, their eyes darting toward the road ahead. Yasmin could hear the distant rumble of a truck engine, the sound growing louder with each passing second. She held her breath, her heart racing as the vehicle drew closer, the fear of being discovered nearly overwhelming.

The truck passed by slowly, its tires kicking up dust as it rumbled down the road. It was an old military vehicle, its once green paint now faded and covered in dirt, the insignia barely visible. Soldiers sat in the back, their rifles slung over their shoulders, their faces hard and unyielding. Yasmin's stomach twisted with fear as she pressed herself closer to the wall, praying they wouldn't be seen.

As the truck disappeared around the corner, Omar let out a slow breath, his body relaxing slightly. "We'll rest here for the night," he said quietly, his voice strained with exhaustion. "It's too dangerous to keep moving after dark."

Yasmin nodded, though the thought of stopping for the night filled her with dread. The streets were no place to rest, especially not in the middle of a war zone. But they had no choice. They were all too weak, too exhausted to keep going.

They huddled together behind the wall, their bodies pressed close for warmth and comfort. The night was cold, the air sharp and biting as it whipped through the broken buildings. Yasmin wrapped her arms around Khaled, pulling him close as he shivered against her. Hassan sat beside her, his face pale and drawn, his eyes wide with fear. Their mother sat on the other side, her hands trembling as she muttered soft prayers under her breath, her voice barely audible over the howling wind.

Omar sat a short distance away, his back against the wall, his eyes scanning the street for any sign of danger. He hadn't spoken much since they had left the refugee camp, his face a mask of grim determination. Yasmin knew he was carrying the weight of their survival on his shoulders, and it was beginning to take its toll.

"Try to sleep," Omar said softly, his voice barely above a whisper. "We'll need our strength for tomorrow."

Yasmin nodded, though she knew sleep wouldn't come easily. Her mind was a whirlwind of fear and grief, the memories of everything they had lost swirling together in a haze of exhaustion. But she forced her eyes to close, knowing that rest was the only thing that could keep her going.

The next morning, Yasmin woke to the sound of distant explosions, the ground trembling beneath her as the shockwaves rolled through the city. Her heart pounded in her chest as she sat up, her body stiff and sore from the night spent on the cold, hard ground. Omar was already awake, his face set in a grim expression as he crouched low, his eyes scanning the street.

"They're getting closer," he muttered, his voice tight with worry. "We need to move. Now."

Yasmin nodded, quickly helping her mother and brothers to their feet. Her body ached with every movement, her muscles stiff and unyielding from the cold and hunger. Khaled stumbled as he stood, his legs trembling beneath him, and Yasmin reached out to steady him, her heart aching at the sight of his pale, gaunt face.

"We're almost there," she whispered, though she wasn't sure if she was trying to reassure him or herself. "Just a little further."

Omar led the way, his pace brisk as they moved through the narrow streets, sticking to the shadows and avoiding the open areas where they might be seen. The sound of gunfire echoed in the distance, growing louder with each passing moment, and Yasmin's heart raced with fear. They had to keep moving. They had to stay ahead of the violence.

But even as they pressed on, Yasmin could feel the weight of exhaustion bearing down on her. Her legs felt like lead, her vision blurring as dizziness overtook her. She stumbled more than once, her body struggling to keep up with the pace, but she forced herself to keep going, driven by the knowledge that stopping meant death.

The streets were eerily quiet, the once vibrant city now reduced to a wasteland of crumbling buildings and shattered glass. The smell of smoke and burning wood hung heavy in the air, a constant reminder of the destruction that had ravaged Gaza. Yasmin kept her head down, her eyes focused on the ground as they walked, trying to block out the horrors that surrounded them.

They had been walking for hours when they came across a small, bombed-out building that offered some semblance of shelter. Omar motioned

for them to stop, his face pale with exhaustion as he sank down onto the ground, his body trembling with fatigue.

"We'll rest here for a while," he said quietly, his voice hoarse. "But we can't stay long."

Yasmin nodded, her body too weak to argue. She collapsed onto the ground beside Khaled, pulling him close as he shivered against her. Her mother sat nearby, her face pale and drawn, her hands trembling as she tried to comfort Hassan, who had grown quieter and more withdrawn with each passing day.

The hunger was a constant ache in Yasmin's belly, gnawing at her insides with an intensity that was impossible to ignore. They hadn't eaten in days, and what little water they had left was barely enough to wet their lips. Yasmin's throat was so dry it hurt to swallow, and her body felt weak, her limbs trembling with exhaustion. She knew they couldn't keep going like this much longer.

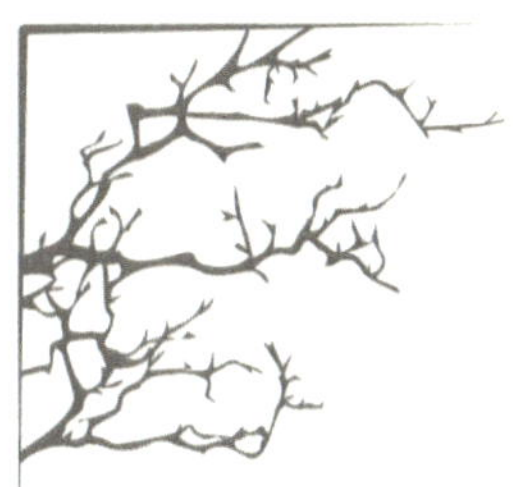

Chapter 6

Omar's Death

The journey had become a slow march through hell. Every step Yasmin took felt like it weighed a thousand pounds, her body dragged down by exhaustion, hunger, and the crushing despair that had settled over her family like a thick, suffocating fog. The war, relentless and unforgiving, had stripped away everything they once held dear—their home, their safety, their father. Now, it threatened to take even more.

Omar had always been the strongest among them. He carried the weight of the world on his shoulders, taking on the role of protector after their father's death, guiding them through the war-torn streets of Gaza with a determination that never seemed to waver. But even the strongest can only endure so much.

The past few weeks had taken a toll on Omar that Yasmin could see but not fully understand. His once vibrant eyes had grown dull, and the strong, steady frame of her brother was now gaunt, his skin stretched thin over his bones. He rarely spoke, his energy focused solely on their survival. It seemed as though he had taken all their pain, all their fear, and shouldered it alone, leaving nothing for himself.

But it wasn't sustainable. No one could carry such a burden for so long without eventually breaking.

The day started like any other in the brutal, war-ravaged land that had become their reality. Yasmin woke to the sound of distant gunfire, her heart racing before her mind could catch up. Omar was already awake, crouched by the broken window of the bombed-out building they had taken refuge in for the night. His silhouette was outlined by the pale morning light filtering through the cracks in the walls.

They had been on the move for weeks now, making their way through the desolate streets, avoiding soldiers, snipers, and the constant threat of airstrikes. The refugee camp in Rafah had offered them brief respite, but it had quickly become a place of chaos and danger, overrun with people just as desperate as they were. The aid trucks had stopped coming, and violence had erupted as people fought over the dwindling supplies. It was no longer a safe place, so they had fled once again, hoping to find somewhere—anywhere—that could offer them a chance at survival.

But Gaza was a warzone. There were no safe places left.

"Get ready," Omar said quietly, his voice barely above a whisper. He turned toward Yasmin, his face ashen and gaunt. "We need to keep moving."

Yasmin nodded, pulling herself up from the cold, hard ground. Her muscles screamed in protest, her body weak from lack of food and water. She glanced at her mother, Aaliyah , who sat in the corner, her eyes closed in silent prayer. Hassan and Khaled, her younger brothers, huddled beside her, their faces pale and drawn, their bodies frail from weeks of starvation.

They were all suffering, but they had no choice but to continue. The alternative—staying in one place, waiting for the war to catch up to them—was unthinkable.

As they gathered their few belongings and prepared to leave, Yasmin noticed the way Omar swayed slightly when he stood, as if his body was struggling to keep him upright. She watched him carefully, her stomach twisting with concern. He had always been the one to keep them moving, to make the difficult decisions that none of them were capable of making. But now, Yasmin could see the cracks in his armour. He was tired—so very tired.

"Omar," she whispered, stepping closer to him. "Maybe we should rest a little longer. You're not well. None of us are."

Omar shook his head, his eyes flicking to the door as if he could sense the danger lurking outside. "We can't afford to stay here. It's not safe. We need to keep going."

Yasmin wanted to argue, to beg him to stop pushing himself so hard, but she knew it would be pointless. Omar wouldn't listen. He had made it his mission to keep them all safe, and he wouldn't stop until they were out of danger—if that was even possible.

Reluctantly, Yasmin nodded, and they set out once again, slipping through the ruins of the city like ghosts, their footsteps barely making a sound as they moved through the crumbling streets. The air was thick with smoke, the acrid scent of burning wood and rubber filling their lungs. The distant sounds of explosions and gunfire were a constant reminder that the war was never far away.

As they walked, Yasmin kept a close eye on Omar, watching the way his shoulders slumped, the way his steps seemed to drag more than usual. He had always been the strong one, the one who could keep going no matter what, but now it seemed like he was running on fumes, his body barely holding together under the strain.

They moved through the day in silence, each of them lost in their own thoughts, too tired to speak. The hunger gnawed at Yasmin's stomach, a constant, aching reminder of how little they had left. Their supplies had dwindled to almost nothing—a few scraps of bread, a small bottle of water that they were rationing carefully. It wasn't enough. It would never be enough.

By late afternoon, the sun hung low in the sky, casting long shadows across the desolate landscape. The streets were eerily quiet, the once vibrant city now reduced to rubble and ash. They hadn't seen another person for hours, and the oppressive silence weighed heavily on Yasmin's chest, making it hard to breathe.

They came across a small, abandoned building that looked like it had once been a shop. Its windows were shattered, and the door hung crooked on its hinges, but it seemed sturdy enough to offer some shelter for the night.

"We'll stop here," Omar said, his voice hoarse. He leaned against the wall, his face pale and drawn. Yasmin could see the dark circles under his eyes, the way his hands shook as he wiped the sweat from his brow.

She reached out to steady him, her heart pounding with fear. "Omar, you're not well. You need to rest."

He shook his head, pushing her hand away gently. "I'm fine," he insisted, though the strain in his voice betrayed him. "We all need to rest."

Yasmin didn't argue, but she knew something was wrong. Omar had been pushing himself too hard for too long, and now his body was beginning to give out. She watched him carefully as they settled inside the building, her stomach twisting with worry.

BENEATH THE ASHES A TESTAMENT OF FAITH

That night, as the others slept, Yasmin sat awake, her mind racing with fear and uncertainty. The hunger gnawed at her insides, but it was nothing compared to the ache in her heart. She had already lost her father, and now she was terrified that she was losing Omar too.

She glanced over at her brother, who lay slumped against the wall, his chest rising and falling in shallow, labored breaths. His face was pale, his skin slick with sweat, and his hands trembled even in sleep.

Yasmin's heart clenched with fear. She couldn't lose him. Not Omar. He was the only thing keeping them together, the only one who knew how to survive in this nightmare. Without him, they would be lost.

As the night dragged on, Omar's condition worsened. His breathing became more labored, his body shaking with fever. Yasmin tried to rouse him, but he barely responded, his eyes glassy and unfocused.

Panic surged through her. "Omar, please," she whispered, her voice trembling with fear. "You have to wake up. You have to keep fighting."

But Omar was slipping away, his body finally giving in to the weeks of exhaustion, hunger, and the relentless stress of keeping his family safe. Yasmin's mind raced, searching for a solution, but there was nothing she could do. They had no medicine, no food, no water. The war had taken everything from them, and now it was taking Omar too.

Tears streamed down her face as she cradled her brother's head in her lap, her heart breaking with each ragged breath he took. She prayed silently, begging Allah to spare him, to give him the strength to survive. But deep down, she knew it was too late.

In the early hours of the morning, Omar's breathing slowed, each breath coming in shallow, labored gasps. Yasmin held him tightly, her tears falling onto his fevered skin as she whispered words of comfort, though she knew he couldn't hear her.

"I'm sorry, Omar," she whispered, her voice breaking. "I'm so sorry."

Omar's hand twitched weakly in hers, and for a moment, Yasmin thought he was trying to speak. She leaned closer, her heart pounding in her chest, but no words came. He was slipping away, and there was nothing she could do to stop it.

As the first light of dawn began to filter through the cracks in the walls, Omar took his final breath. His body went still, his hand falling limp in Yasmin's grasp.

A sob tore from Yasmin's throat as she clutched her brother's lifeless body to her chest, her heart shattering into a million pieces. She had lost him. The war had taken him from her, just as it had taken their father, their home, their safety.

For a long time, Yasmin sat there, holding Omar's body, her tears falling silently onto his skin. She didn't know how long she sat there, her mind numb with grief, her body trembling with exhaustion. The world around her felt distant, as if she were trapped in a nightmare she couldn't wake up from.

Eventually, she became aware of her mother's soft sobs beside her. Aaliyah had woken and found them, her eyes wide with horror as she realized what had happened. Hassan and Khaled stood nearby, their faces pale and stricken, their eyes filled with the same fear and grief that weighed so heavily on Yasmin's heart.

They had lost Omar. And now, they were truly lost.

The days that followed were a blur of grief and numbness. Yasmin could barely function, her body moving through the motions of survival on autopilot, her mind too consumed by the loss of her brother to fully comprehend the world around her. She couldn't eat, couldn't sleep. The hunger gnawed at her insides, but it was nothing compared to the pain in her heart.

Omar had been their rock, their protector. He had kept them safe, had guided them through the worst of the war, had made the impossible decisions that none of them could. And now, he was gone. Yasmin didn't know how they would survive without him.

Her mother was a shell of the woman she had once been, her eyes hollow and vacant as she sat in silence, clutching her prayer beads in her trembling hands. Hassan and Khaled were quiet, their once lively spirits dampened by the loss of their brother. The family that had once been so close, so full of love and laughter, had been shattered by the war, and Yasmin didn't know if they would ever be whole again.

They buried Omar in a small patch of dirt outside the building where he had died, marking his grave with a simple stone. There were no words spoken, no prayers said. They didn't have the strength for it. Yasmin stood over his grave, her heart breaking as she stared down at the freshly turned earth, her mind racing with the memories of the brother she had loved so deeply.

"I'm sorry," she whispered, her voice trembling with grief. "I'm so sorry, Omar."

But her words felt hollow, empty. Nothing she said or did could bring him back. Nothing could undo the pain and suffering that had led them to this moment.

The war had taken everything from them. And now, it had taken Omar too.

In the days that followed Omar's death, Yasmin found herself lost in a fog of grief and despair. The world around her felt distant, as if she were moving through a dream, her body disconnected from her mind. She barely spoke, barely ate. The hunger that gnawed at her belly had become a dull ache, overshadowed by the pain in her heart.

She tried to comfort her mother, but Aaliyah was a shadow of the woman she had once been. She had lost her husband and now her eldest son, and the grief had hollowed her out, leaving her. fragile and broken. Hassan and Khaled clung to Yasmin, their once playful spirits now subdued by the weight of their loss.

They continued to move, but it was aimless. Without Omar to guide them, they were lost—both physically and emotionally. They wandered through the war-torn streets of Gaza, their footsteps heavy with exhaustion, their hearts weighed down by the unbearable pain of losing Omar. Each day felt like a lifetime, every hour a struggle to keep going.

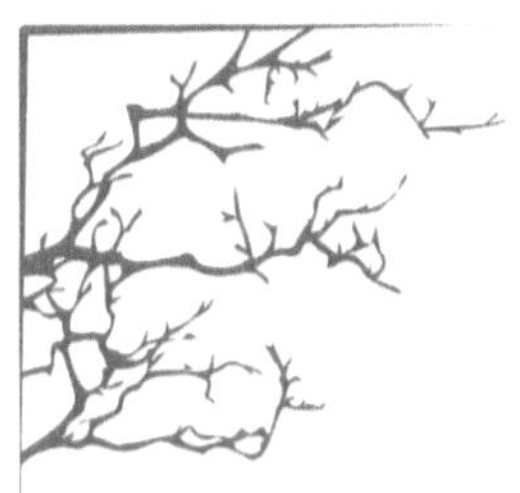

Chapter 7

Allah's Blessing

The days that followed Omar's death were filled with unimaginable despair. Yasmin's family was barely surviving, trapped in a state of perpetual hunger, exhaustion, and grief. Without Omar's leadership and strength, they felt adrift in a world that had been ravaged by war. Each step forward was a painful reminder of all they had lost, and every night was a struggle to stay alive.

Yasmin could feel the weight of responsibility pressing down on her. She was now the oldest, the one her mother and younger brothers depended on. Omar had protected them, but now that he was gone, it was up to her. Yet the burden seemed too much to bear. She felt hollow, lost in her grief, her body weak from starvation, and her heart aching with loss.

Her mother, Aaliyah , had grown more frail with each passing day. She spoke less and less, her prayers barely more than whispers as she clutched her prayer beads with trembling hands. Khaled and Hassan, too, were growing weaker. The light in their eyes had dimmed, their once playful spirits now subdued by hunger and the unbearable grief of losing their father and brother.

Food had become a distant memory. The hunger gnawed at them constantly, an ever-present ache that left them weak and dizzy. Yasmin had searched desperately for food, but the war had consumed everything. The markets had long been abandoned, and any stores or homes they passed were empty, stripped bare by others who were just as desperate to survive. Water, too, was scarce. The small bottle they had carried with them was now empty, and each drop they had rationed had barely been enough to wet their parched lips.

Yasmin had never felt so helpless.

Days turned into weeks, and the situation grew more dire. Yasmin's body had become little more than skin and bones, her energy drained by the endless hunger. Her mother, too, was wasting away, her once strong hands now weak and trembling. Khaled and Hassan barely had the strength to stand, their small bodies frail and emaciated. Yasmin tried to hide her fear from them, but the look in their eyes told her they knew. They all knew.

There was a part of Yasmin that wanted to give up. To surrender to the despair that had taken root in her heart. She had already lost so much—her father, Omar, their home, their way of life. What was left for them? The war showed no signs of ending, and with no food or water, they wouldn't last much longer. But even in her darkest moments, Yasmin held on to one thing: her faith.

Every night, as they huddled together for warmth, Yasmin prayed. She prayed to Allah for strength, for guidance, for mercy. She prayed for the souls of her father and Omar, that they had found peace in the afterlife. And she prayed for her family, that somehow, some way, they would survive this nightmare.

"Please, Allah," she whispered one night, tears streaming down her face as she clutched her prayer beads. "I don't know how much longer we can go on like this. Please, guide us. Help us. We need Your mercy."

Her voice broke, her body trembling with grief and exhaustion. But even as her tears fell, she held on to her faith. She had to believe that Allah was watching over them, that He had a plan for them. It was all she had left.

It was just before dawn when Yasmin felt the first drops of rain on her skin.

She had been sitting outside, staring blankly at the horizon, too weak and exhausted to sleep. The night had been unusually quiet, the distant sounds of gunfire and explosions absent for the first time in weeks. The sky had been overcast, a thick blanket of clouds covering the stars, but there had been no sign of rain.

But then, out of nowhere, the rain began to fall.

At first, it was just a light drizzle, barely more than a mist. But within minutes, it grew heavier, the drops falling faster and harder, drenching the dry earth beneath her feet. Yasmin blinked in disbelief as the cool water soaked through her clothes, her mind struggling to comprehend what was happening. She had prayed for a miracle, but she hadn't expected this.

She looked up at the sky, her eyes filling with tears as the rain continued to pour down. "Thank you, Allah," she whispered, her voice barely audible over the sound of the rain. "Thank you."

She rushed inside the small, crumbling building where her family was huddled together, her heart pounding with excitement. "Mama, wake up! It's raining!"

Her mother stirred, her eyes blinking open in confusion. Khaled and Hassan, too, slowly sat up, their faces pale and drawn, their bodies weak from hunger and dehydration.

"Rain?" Aaliyah murmured, her voice hoarse. She hadn't heard the sound of rain in weeks, not since the war had begun.

"Yes, rain!" Yasmin said, her voice filled with hope. "We can collect it! We can drink it!"

The realization seemed to spark something in her mother's eyes, a glimmer of hope that had long been absent. Together, they rushed outside, their hands cupped to catch the falling water. It wasn't much, but it was enough. Enough to wet their lips, to ease the dryness in their throats. Enough to give them hope.

Yasmin found an old, rusted tin can in the rubble and held it out to collect more of the rainwater. Her heart pounded with gratitude as she watched the can slowly fill. It wasn't clean, it wasn't perfect, but it was water—precious, life-saving water.

For the first time in weeks, Yasmin felt hope stir in her chest. Maybe this was a sign. Allah will never abandoned them after all.

The rain continued to fall throughout the day, a steady, gentle shower that soaked the parched earth and brought relief to Yasmin and her family. They took turns drinking from the can, rationing the water carefully, knowing they couldn't waste a single drop. It wasn't enough to sustain them for long, but it was a gift, a blessing, and for that, Yasmin was grateful.

That night, as they huddled together in their small shelter, Yasmin prayed once more, this time with renewed hope. "Thank you, Allah," she whispered, her voice trembling with emotion. "Thank you for this blessing. Please, continue to watch over us. We need Your guidance, now more than ever."

Her mother joined her in prayer, her soft voice filling the space around them. Even Hassan and Khaled, weak as they were, bowed their heads, their small hands clasped together as they whispered their own prayers. It was a moment of peace, a moment of connection to something greater than themselves, and it filled Yasmin's heart with a warmth she hadn't felt in a long time.

The following morning, the rain had stopped, but the air was cool and fresh, the earth damp beneath their feet. Yasmin felt a renewed sense of purpose as she stood outside, the cool breeze brushing against her skin. The rain had been a gift, a sign that they were not alone, and it had given her the strength to keep going.

They continued their journey, moving slowly through the ruined streets of Gaza, their bodies still weak from hunger but their spirits bolstered by the rain. Yasmin kept her eyes on the horizon, searching for any sign of food, of aid, of something—anything—that could help them survive.

It was late in the afternoon when they came across a small, abandoned market. The building had been partially destroyed by an airstrike, its roof caved in and its windows shattered. But as Yasmin stepped inside, her heart skipped a beat.

There, among the rubble and debris, was a sack of flour, half-buried beneath the fallen beams.

Yasmin rushed forward, her hands trembling as she pulled the sack free. It wasn't much—just a small, tattered sack, its contents likely old and stale. But it was food. Actual food.

Her mother gasped as she saw what Yasmin had found, her eyes filling with tears. "Thank you, Allah," she whispered, her hands clasped together in gratitude.

Yasmin smiled through her own tears, her heart pounding with relief. They had found food. It wasn't much, but it was enough to keep them going, to give them the strength they so desperately needed.

They gathered around the small fire they had built outside the market, using the flour to make flatbread. It was simple, barely more than water and flour mixed together and cooked over the flames, but to Yasmin, it tasted like the finest meal she had ever had. The warmth of the bread filled her belly, easing the hunger that had gnawed at her for so long.

As they ate, Yasmin felt a sense of peace settle over her. The war was still raging around them, the future still uncertain. But in that moment, they were together. They had food, they had water, and they had each other.

And they had their faith.

"Allah has blessed us," her mother said softly, her voice filled with emotion. "He has given us what we need to survive."

Yasmin nodded, her heart swelling with gratitude. "Yes," she whispered. "He has."

The days that followed were still difficult, but Yasmin and her family found renewed strength in the blessings they had received. The sack of flour provided them with food for several days, and they managed to find more rainwater to drink. It wasn't much, but it was enough to keep them going.

Yasmin knew that they still had a long way to go. The war showed no signs of ending, and their future was still uncertain. But for the first time in a long time, she felt hope. Hope that they would survive. Hope that they would find a way through this nightmare.

As they continued their journey, Yasmin held on to her faith, knowing that Allah was watching over them. He had blessed them with food and water when they needed it most, and she knew that He would continue to guide them.

"Allah is with us," she whispered one night as they huddled together for warmth. "He will see us through this."

Her mother smiled softly, her eyes filled with the same quiet strength that Yasmin had always admired. "Yes," she said. "He will."

And as Yasmin closed her eyes and let sleep take her, she held on to that belief, knowing that no matter what the future held, they were not alone.

The weeks that followed were still filled with hardship. The war had not abated, and they were still living in a world consumed by violence and uncertainty. But Yasmin and her family had found a new strength, a new resolve to keep going.

They continued to move from place to place, always searching for food, for water, for safety. It wasn't easy, and there were days when the hunger and exhaustion threatened to overwhelm them. But they held on, driven by the belief that Allah was watching over them, guiding them through the darkness.

Yasmin became the leader of their small family, taking on the role that Omar had once held. It wasn't a role she had asked for, but it was one she accepted with quiet determination. She knew that her mother and brothers were depending on her, and she couldn't let them down.

And so, she kept going. She kept searching for food, for water, for safety. She kept praying, her faith in Allah unshaken, even in the face of unimaginable hardship.

It was on one of these journeys, as they made their way through the ruins of a small village, that they came across a group of aid workers.

Yasmin's heart leaped in her chest as she saw them, their bright vests a stark contrast to the desolate landscape around them. They were handing out food and water to a small crowd of refugees, and Yasmin felt tears fill her eyes as she realized what this meant.

Help had finally come.

She rushed forward, her legs trembling with exhaustion, but her heart pounding with hope. The aid workers welcomed her and her family, offering them food, water, and blankets. It was more than they had had in weeks, and Yasmin couldn't stop the tears that streamed down her face as she accepted their kindness.

Alhamdulillah "Thank you," she whispered, her voice trembling with emotion. "Thank you so much."

One of the aid workers smiled kindly at her, his eyes filled with compassion. "You're welcome. We're here to help."

Yasmin nodded, her heart swelling with gratitude. For the first time in months, she felt truly safe.

As they sat together, eating the food they had been given, Yasmin closed her eyes and whispered a prayer of thanks.

"Thank you, Allah," she whispered. "Thank you for guiding us, for protecting us. Thank you for this blessing."

Her mother, sitting beside her, placed a hand on her shoulder, her eyes filled with tears of gratitude.

And as Yasmin looked around at her family, at the food and water they had been given, at the aid workers who had come to help them, she knew that they had been blessed.

Allah had answered their prayers.

And in that moment, Yasmin knew that no matter what happened next, they would survive.

Because Allah was with them.

He always had been.

And He always would be.

The months that followed were filled with challenges, but Yasmin and her family continued to survive, buoyed by the blessings they had received. The war was still a constant presence, and the future was still uncertain, but they had found a new strength in their faith.

Because of malnutrition baby Aaliyah passed way and they have a given a proper burial for her within the camp site.

They continued to move from place to place, finding refuge where they could, and accepting help from the aid workers who had become a lifeline for so many. Yasmin had learned to be resourceful, to adapt to the ever-changing circumstances of their lives. But through it all, she never lost sight of the one thing that had kept them going: their faith in Allah.

There were still days when the hunger and exhaustion threatened to overwhelm them, when the weight of their grief and loss felt too heavy to bear. But Yasmin had learned to carry that weight, to find strength in her faith and in the love of her family.

Her mother, though still frail, had found peace in her prayers, and her quiet strength was a source of comfort to Yasmin and her brothers. Hassan and Khaled had begun to smile again, their spirits slowly returning as they adjusted to their new reality.

They had lost so much, but they had each other. And they had their faith.

And that was enough.

As they continued their journey, Yasmin knew that there would be more challenges ahead, more hardships to endure. But she also knew that they would survive.

Because Allah was with them.

And that was all they needed.

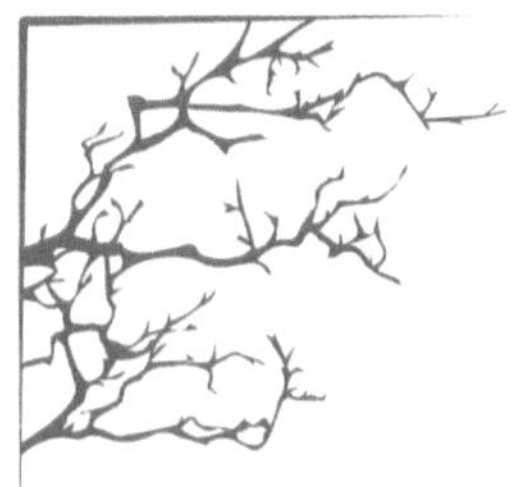

Chapter 8

Love Amidst the Rubble

The refugee camp in Rafah had become Yasmin's new reality, a place where time seemed to stand still, suspended between the horrors of war and the fragile hope of survival. The camp was crowded, filled with people who had lost everything—families separated by violence, children orphaned, homes reduced to rubble. Yet amidst the suffering, there were moments of resilience, of kindness, of community. Yasmin had learned that even in the darkest of times, humanity had a way of finding light.

It had been months since she and her family had found refuge in the camp. Life was hard, but it was at least safer than the constant barrage of gunfire and airstrikes that had ravaged Gaza. The tents were flimsy, the food scarce, and the water rationed, but there was a rhythm to their days now. Yasmin had grown used to the struggle, to the daily queues for bread and the cold nights huddled together with her mother and brothers under a thin blanket. She had learned to find peace in prayer, comfort in the small victories—another day survived, another meal shared.

But even in this bleak environment, something had shifted. Life, no matter how harsh, always found a way to bloom again.

It was in this dusty, crowded camp that Yasmin reunited with an old friend, a boy she had known before the war had upended their lives Muhammad.

Yasmin hadn't thought of Muhammad in years. He had been a childhood friend, someone she had grown up with in the same neighbourhood before the war tore everything apart. They had shared innocent conversations in the coffee shop her father used to run, laughing as children often do, unaware of the looming future that awaited them. Back then, the world had felt much simpler, full of possibility. Muhammad had been kind, always smiling, his eyes bright with curiosity and hope.

When she first saw him again in Rafah, her heart skipped a beat. He had changed, of course—war had that effect on everyone—but there was still something of the boy she remembered in the man who now stood before her.

She had been helping distribute bread at the food station when she saw him. He was standing in line, taller than she remembered, his face gaunt from the hardship of war but his eyes the same deep brown she had always known. For a moment, Yasmin thought she was imagining things. It seemed impossible that someone from her past could reappear in this chaotic place.

"Muhammad?" she whispered, her voice trembling with disbelief.

He turned at the sound of his name, his eyes scanning the crowd until they landed on her. His expression shifted from confusion to recognition, and then his face broke into a wide smile.

"Yasmin," he said softly, as if saying her name brought back a flood of memories. He stepped forward, his smile faltering for a moment as he took in her appearance, her thin frame, her tired eyes. "I can't believe it's you."

Yasmin felt her heart swell with emotion. She had lost so much, endured so much, that the sight of Muhammad felt like a small miracle, a reminder of the life she had once known.

They embraced awkwardly, as if unsure of how to navigate the gap of years and war that lay between them. But the moment they spoke, it was as though no time had passed at all.

"I thought I'd never see you again," Yasmin said, her voice thick with emotion.

"I thought the same," Muhammad replied. "After the war started, everything just... fell apart."

Yasmin nodded, the weight of all they had lost hanging heavy between them. But despite the sadness, there was something comforting in seeing him again. It was like finding a piece of her old life amidst the ruins of the new one.

Over the next few weeks, Yasmin and Muhammad grew closer. He had lost his entire family to the war, his parents killed in an airstrike that had levelled their home. He had survived by sheer luck, moving from place to place, eventually finding his way to the refugee camp in Rafah. Their shared grief brought them together, but so did their shared hope. They were both survivors, and in each other, they found a refuge from the despair that often threatened to consume them.

They spent long hours talking about their past, about their childhood in Gaza before the war. They spoke of their families, of the dreams they once had, and of the lives they had hoped to live. But as time passed, their conversations shifted. It wasn't just the past that connected them anymore—it was the future. In a place where hope was scarce, they found it in each other.

Yasmin felt something she hadn't felt in a long time: a flicker of happiness. It was fragile, easily overshadowed by the harshness of their reality, but it was there, growing slowly each time she and Muhammad were together.

One afternoon, as the sun dipped low over the camp, casting everything in a golden light, Muhammad took Yasmin's hand.

"I never thought I'd find something good in all this," he said quietly, his eyes searching hers. "But I found you."

Yasmin's heart fluttered, her chest tight with emotions she hadn't allowed herself to feel for so long. Love was something she had buried deep inside her, too focused on survival to think about it. But now, standing with Muhammad in the midst of so much loss and pain, she realized that love was exactly what she needed. It was what they all needed.

"I don't want to lose you again," Muhammad continued, his voice trembling with the weight of his words. "I know this isn't the life we dreamed of, but I want to spend whatever time we have left together. Will you marry me, Yasmin?"

Tears welled in Yasmin's eyes, not from sadness but from the overwhelming feeling of hope. She nodded, unable to speak at first, her heart full.

"Yes," she whispered, finally finding her voice. "I'll marry you."

The decision to marry in the refugee camp was not an easy one. There was no grand celebration, no beautiful venue, no expensive wedding dress. But for Yasmin and Muhammad, it didn't matter. They had found each other in the midst of the rubble, and that was all they needed. Their love was a defiant act of hope, a way to reclaim some joy in a world that had taken so much from them.

Word of their wedding spread quickly through the camp, and the entire community came together to make the occasion as special as possible. The people of Rafah, despite their own suffering, were eager to help. Some donated small pieces of fabric to create a simple dress for Yasmin, while others brought whatever food they could spare for the wedding feast. It wasn't much, but it was enough to show that even in the darkest of times, there was still room for love, for happiness.

The day of the wedding dawned with clear skies, a rare break from the gloom that often hung over the camp. Yasmin dressed in the simple white gown that had been sewn for her by some of the women in the camp, her heart pounding with nervous excitement. Her mother, Aaliyah , stood beside her, tears in her eyes as she helped adjust the fabric.

"You look beautiful," Aaliyah whispered, her voice filled with emotion.

Yasmin smiled, her heart swelling with gratitude. For so long, she had wondered if there would ever be a day when she could feel happiness again. But now, standing on the threshold of her new life with Muhammad, she felt a sense of peace she hadn't known in years.

When she stepped out of the tent, the entire camp was waiting for her. People had gathered to witness the wedding, their faces filled with joy and hope. It was a small celebration, but in the midst of so much sorrow, it felt like a miracle.

Muhammad stood at the front, waiting for her with a smile that melted her heart. His eyes were filled with love, and Yasmin felt her own heart swell with emotion as she walked toward him.

The ceremony was simple, but it was perfect. They exchanged vows under the open sky, surrounded by the people of Rafah who had become like family to them. As they spoke their promises to each other, the sound of laughter and joy filled the air—a rare and precious thing in a place so often filled with the sounds of war.

For a brief moment, the war didn't exist. There was only love, only the joy of two people who had found each other in the midst of the rubble.

After the ceremony, the people of Rafah gathered to celebrate. They shared the simple meal that had been prepared, and for the first time in what felt like forever, the camp was filled with laughter and music. Children danced, their bare feet kicking up dust as they twirled in circles, their smiles bright and full of life. The adults clapped along, their faces glowing with happiness.

Yasmin and Muhammad sat together, hand in hand, watching the scene unfold around them. It was a small wedding, held in the most unlikely of places, but it was filled with more love and joy than Yasmin had ever imagined.

"I never thought we'd have this," Yasmin whispered, resting her head on Muhammad's shoulder. "Not here, not like this."

Muhammad smiled, his arm wrapping around her waist. "It's not what we imagined, but it's ours. And that's enough. "Alhamdulillah.

Yasmin nodded, her heart full of gratitude for this moment, for this love that had blossomed in the midst of so much pain.

As the sun set over Rafah, casting the sky in shades of pink and orange, Yasmin closed her eyes and whispered a prayer of thanks.

"Thank you, Allah," she whispered. "Thank you for bringing us together."

And as the stars began to twinkle in the night sky, Yasmin knew that despite the war, despite the loss, she had found something beautiful. She had found love.

And that was the greatest gift of all.

In the days that followed the wedding, Yasmin and Muhammad settled into their new life together, finding solace in each other's arms. The war was still a constant presence, and life in the camp remained difficult, but they faced it together, their love a source of strength that helped them endure the hardships that lay ahead.

For the people of Rafah, the wedding had been a beacon of hope, a reminder that even in the midst of war, there was still room for love, for joy, for life. The memory of that day lingered in the camp, a precious moment of happiness that could not be taken away.

Yasmin and Muhammad knew that the road ahead would not be easy. The war was far from over, and there were still many challenges to face. But they faced them together, their hearts full of love and their faith in Allah unshaken.

And as long as they had each other, they knew they could survive anything.

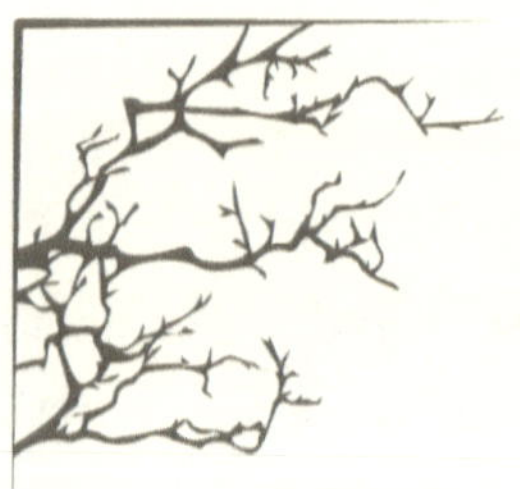

Chapter 9

A Final Farewell

The days following Yasmin and Muhammad's wedding were filled with a bittersweet sense of normalcy, the kind of peace they had almost forgotten was possible. Love had found its way through the cracks of war, and for a brief time, Yasmin allowed herself to believe that despite everything, they might be able to build a life amidst the ruins. The refugee camp in Rafah had become their home, and though the hardships were endless, the love she shared with Muhammad gave her the strength to face each day.

But as the days turned into weeks, a shadow began to creep over Yasmin's heart—a shadow that had nothing to do with the war raging outside the camp.

Her mother, Aaliyah , had been growing weaker for some time, though she tried to hide it. Yasmin could see it in the way her mother's steps had slowed, the way her hands shook when she worked, the paleness of her skin. At first, Yasmin dismissed it as exhaustion. After all, they were all worn down by the endless struggle for survival, and the stress of living through war had taken its toll on every member of their family. But as the days passed, it became clear that something was terribly wrong.

Aaliyah 's cough, which had started as a minor annoyance, soon deepened into a ragged, relentless hacking that left her gasping for breath. Her once-strong voice, the voice that had comforted Yasmin through the darkest times, grew thin and hoarse. She became feverish, her body wracked with chills that no blanket could soothe.

Yasmin watched helplessly as her mother's condition worsened, her heart heavy with dread. The camp had little in the way of medical supplies, and with the borders closed and aid shipments blocked, there was no way to get the medicine or care that her mother so desperately needed. What little aid did make it into Rafah was distributed sparingly, and the most vulnerable—the elderly, the children—often received priority. There simply wasn't enough to go around.

Yasmin tried everything she could think of to ease her mother's suffering. She gave her what little food they had, made sure she was warm at night, and prayed constantly for Allah to show them mercy. But no matter what Yasmin did, her mother's condition continued to deteriorate.

It wasn't just the illness that haunted Yasmin—it was the feeling of helplessness that came with it. The war had taken so much from them, but this—this felt like the cruellest blow of all. To watch her mother, who had endured so much, slowly slip away without the medical care that could save her... It was unbearable.

One morning, as the weak sunlight filtered through the cracks in their tent, Yasmin sat beside her mother, her heart heavy with worry. Aaliyah lay on the small mat they had fashioned for her, her chest rising and falling unevenly as she struggled to catch her breath. Her face was pale, her skin damp with sweat, and her once-bright eyes were clouded with exhaustion and pain.

"Mama," Yasmin whispered, her voice trembling as she took her mother's hand in hers. "I'm going to find help. There must be something I can do. Someone in the camp must have medicine."

But Aaliyah 's grip tightened weakly on Yasmin's hand, her eyes opening just a sliver. "No, Yasmin," she rasped, her voice so faint that Yasmin had to lean in to hear. "Don't... waste your strength. There's... nothing they can do."

Tears welled up in Yasmin's eyes as she shook her head, refusing to believe her mother's words. "There has to be something, Mama. We can't just give up."

Aaliyah 's lips curved into a faint, tired smile. "My sweet daughter... I'm not giving up. But we must... accept what Allah has written for us."

Yasmin's heart clenched at her mother's words. She had always admired her mother's unwavering faith, her ability to trust in Allah's plan no matter how difficult the circumstances. But this—this was too much. How could she accept losing her mother, the one person who had been her anchor through every storm?

"I can't lose you, Mama," Yasmin whispered, her voice breaking. "Not after everything..."

Aaliyah 's hand trembled as she reached up to touch Yasmin's cheek, her eyes filled with a quiet understanding. "You won't lose me," she murmured. "I will always be with you... in your heart, in your prayers."

Tears spilled down Yasmin's cheeks as she leaned over her mother, her chest aching with the weight of her grief. "I don't know how to do this without you," she whispered.

"You are stronger than you know, my daughter," Aaliyah replied softly. "You have always been strong. Look at all you have survived... You have a good heart, Yasmin, and you are surrounded by love. Muhammad, Hassan, Khaled... they need you. You must be strong for them."

Yasmin closed her eyes, her tears falling onto her mother's hand. She wanted to scream, to rage against the unfairness of it all. But deep down, she knew her mother was right. She had to be strong. For her family, for her husband, for herself.

Over the next few days, Aaliyah grew weaker and weaker, her strength slowly ebbing away. Yasmin stayed by her side, refusing to leave her mother even for a moment. She prayed constantly, her heart filled with a desperate plea for mercy, for a miracle.

But as the days passed, it became clear that nothing going to change and medical aid is also not coming.

One night, as Yasmin sat beside her mother, Muhammad came to join her. He sat quietly, his presence a silent comfort as they watched over Aaliyah together. He had become her rock in these difficult times, his love and support a constant source of strength.

"She's holding on for you," Muhammad said quietly, his voice filled with quiet understanding. "She wants to make sure you're going to be okay."

Yasmin's heart clenched at his words, the weight of her grief almost too much to bear. "I don't know if I will be," she whispered, her voice trembling with emotion.

"You will," Muhammad replied gently, taking her hand in his. "You have your mother's strength, Yasmin. And you have all of us."

Yasmin nodded, though her heart still felt heavy with the weight of what was coming. She didn't know how she would survive this, how she would find the strength to keep going without her mother. But she knew she had to try. For her family, for the love her mother had always shown her.

The end came quietly, in the early hours of the morning.

Yasmin had fallen asleep beside her mother, her head resting on the edge of the mat. She had been too exhausted to stay awake, her body finally giving in to the fatigue that had been building for days. But she woke suddenly, her heart pounding in her chest as if it knew what was happening.

Her mother's breathing had grown shallow, barely more than a whisper of air. Yasmin knelt beside her, her hand trembling as she took her mother's cold fingers in hers.

"Mama," Yasmin whispered, her voice trembling with fear and sorrow.

Aaliyah's eyes fluttered open one last time, and for a brief moment, her gaze was clear and focused. She looked at Yasmin, her lips curling into a faint, peaceful smile.

"Be strong, my love," she whispered. "I am at peace... Allah is with us."

And with that, her chest rose once more before falling still.

Yasmin felt the world fall away, her breath catching in her throat as the reality of her mother's death washed over her. Aaliyah was gone. The woman who had been her constant source of comfort, her guiding light, had slipped away quietly in the night, leaving Yasmin behind in a world that suddenly felt too vast, too empty.

For a moment, Yasmin couldn't move. She couldn't think, couldn't breathe. Her mother's lifeless hand rested in hers, and all she could do was stare at her mother's peaceful face, the face that had smiled at her, cried with her, and shared so many moments of love and strength.

A sob escaped Yasmin's lips, breaking the silence of the early morning. She clutched her mother's hand to her chest, her body shaking with grief as the tears fell freely down her face.

"Mama," she whispered brokenly. "Please..."

But there was no answer. There would never be an answer.

Muhammad, who had been sitting quietly nearby, knelt beside Yasmin, his arms wrapping around her trembling frame. He held her as she wept, his own heart heavy with sorrow.

"We'll get through this," he whispered softly, his voice breaking with emotion. "We'll get through it together."

Yasmin buried her face in Muhammad's chest, her sobs muffled by his embrace. She had lost so much—her father, Omar, and now her mother. The weight of her grief felt unbearable, but Muhammad was right. They had to keep going. Life, even in its cruellest moments, had to continue.

The people of the camp gathered to mourn Aaliyah's passing. They had come to know her quiet strength, her kindness, and her unwavering faith. Though the camp was a place of hardship, the people had become a community, and they shared in Yasmin's grief, offering what little comfort they could.

They wrapped Aaliyah's body in a simple cloth, and together, they carried her to a small patch of earth on the outskirts of the camp. There, beneath the open sky, they laid her to rest. Yasmin knelt beside her mother's grave, her tears falling silently as she whispered a final prayer for her.

"May Allah grant you peace, Mama," Yasmin whispered, her voice trembling. "I love you."

As the sun set over Rafah, Yasmin stood with Muhammad by her side, her heart heavy with sorrow but filled with a quiet strength. Her mother was gone, but she would always be with her—in her heart, in her prayers, in every moment of love and kindness she shared with the world.

And as Yasmin looked up at the darkening sky, the stars beginning to twinkle overhead, she felt a small flicker of hope.

Life would go on. The war would end. And one day, they would all find peace.

Because even in death, her mother had taught her the most important lesson of all: faith and love would always endure.

In the days that followed, Yasmin grieved, but she also found a renewed sense of purpose. Her mother had left her with a legacy of strength, of faith, of love—and now it was Yasmin's responsibility to carry that forward. She would honour her mother by living, by caring for her family, and by holding on to the hope that one day, the war would end, and they would find peace.

She had Muhammad by her side, her brothers, and the memory of her parents to guide her.

And with that, Yasmin knew that no matter how hard the road ahead might be, she would survive.

Because love, faith, and hope were the greatest gifts her mother had given her.

And those gifts would never fade.

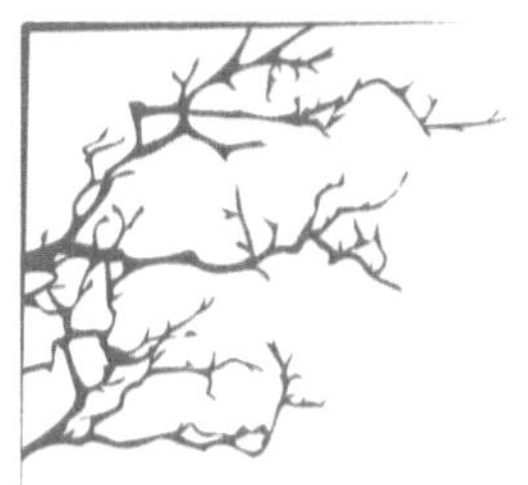

Chapter 10

The Attack on Rafah the safe zone

The war had dragged on for what felt like an eternity. The days blurred together in the endless rhythm of survival, with each day in the refugee camp in Rafah bringing new challenges, new hardships, and new griefs. Yasmin had learned to live with the weight of her losses—her father, Omar, and most recently, her mother. Yet despite the pain that had become a constant companion, she had found a semblance of peace in the small family that remained: her brothers Hassan and Khaled, and her husband, Muhammad.

Life in Rafah was fragile. The camp was overcrowded, and the conditions were harsh, with limited food and water and the constant threat of violence hanging over their heads like a sword that could fall at any moment. But amidst the rubble and the dust, there was still hope. Muhammad had become Yasmin's anchor, his quiet strength helping her navigate the grief of losing her mother. Her younger brothers, though weakened by the hardships of life in the camp, still smiled occasionally, their youthful spirits refusing to be completely extinguished by the war.

Yasmin had also found new purpose, volunteering alongside international aid workers who had come to Rafah to help the refugees. These social helpers had arrived from all corners of the world, bringing with them food, medical supplies, and a deep desire to make a difference. Yasmin had gravitated toward them, drawn by their compassion and their willingness to work tirelessly to help those in need. Through her work with them, Yasmin had found a small sense of control in an uncontrollable world. It felt good to help others, to do something tangible, no matter how small, to alleviate the suffering around her.

That morning, Yasmin had woken with a strange sense of unease. It was a feeling she couldn't quite shake, a gnawing anxiety that had settled in her chest, making it hard to breathe. Muhammad had noticed her discomfort as they shared a small breakfast of bread and water.

"What's wrong?" he had asked, his brow furrowed with concern. "You seem tense."

Yasmin had forced a smile, trying to push aside her worries. "I don't know," she admitted. "It's just... something feels off today."

Muhammad had squeezed her hand, his warmth seeping into her skin. "Don't worry. We're safe here, Yasmin. I know it doesn't always feel like it, but we've made it this far. We'll keep going."

Yasmin had nodded, but the unease lingered in the pit of her stomach, a dark cloud on an otherwise clear morning.

Later that day, Yasmin left the small tent she shared with Muhammad, Hassan, and Khaled to meet with the social workers. She had been volunteering with them for weeks now, helping to distribute food and supplies to the families in the camp. It was difficult work, especially when the resources were so limited, but it gave Yasmin a sense of purpose—something to focus on beyond her grief and fear.

The social workers had gathered near the southern edge of the camp, where they were setting up a temporary clinic to treat the sick and injured. Yasmin had been eager to help, knowing how desperately the people in the camp needed medical care. It was exhausting work, but it was also deeply fulfilling. For a few hours each day, Yasmin could forget about the war, about the losses she had suffered, and focus instead on helping others.

As she worked alongside the aid workers, distributing medicine and bandages to the families who had lined up for help, that sense of unease continued to nag at her. She couldn't explain it, but something felt wrong. It was as if the air itself had changed, thickening with an unspoken tension that pressed down on her chest.

"Are you all right, Yasmin?" one of the social workers, a kind woman named Sarah from France, asked, her voice filled with concern.

Yasmin nodded quickly, not wanting to burden anyone with her worries. "I'm fine," she said, forcing a smile. "Just a little tired."

Sarah smiled sympathetically. "We all are," she said, her voice soft. "But you've been doing such a wonderful job. The people here really appreciate everything you do."

Yasmin thanked her, but the words felt hollow. Her mind was elsewhere, her thoughts drifting back to Muhammad and her brothers. She couldn't shake the feeling that something was wrong.

The attack came without warning.

One moment, Yasmin was helping a mother bandage her son's arm, and the next, the air was filled with the deafening roar of explosions. The ground shook violently beneath her feet, and the sky, which had been clear and bright just moments before, turned black with smoke. The screams of the camp's residents echoed in her ears, blending with the sound of bombs and gunfire.

Yasmin's heart stopped as panic gripped her chest. Her mind raced, her thoughts spinning in a frantic blur as the world around her descended into chaos.

"North Rafah!" someone shouted, their voice barely audible over the noise. "They're bombing the north side!"

The north side. Her heart clenched painfully as she realized what that meant. Muhammad, Hassan,

and Khaled were on the north side of the camp. They had stayed behind at their tent while Yasmin went to help the social workers. She had kissed Muhammad goodbye that morning, feeling the warmth of his hand in hers, telling her brothers she'd be back soon. Now, that simple farewell felt like a knife twisting in her chest.

"No... no, no, no!" Yasmin gasped, her voice trembling as she stumbled forward. Her feet felt heavy, her body unsteady as the explosions continued to shake the earth beneath her. The sky was filled with thick, acrid smoke, making it hard to see, but Yasmin pushed through the chaos, her only thought on getting back to her family.

She could hear the screams of people running, crying for help, but all of it was a blur to her. Her vision narrowed, her heart pounding in her ears as she forced her way through the crowd, her legs trembling with fear. She couldn't think clearly, her mind consumed by a single, desperate thought: **She had to get to them. She had to find them.**

"Yasmin!" Sarah called out, her voice panicked as she grabbed Yasmin's arm. "You can't go that way! It's not safe!"

But Yasmin shook her off, her heart racing. "My family is there," she whispered, her voice breaking. "I have to go."

Sarah's eyes were wide with fear, but she let go of Yasmin, understanding the urgency in her voice. "Be careful!" she shouted after her, but Yasmin was already moving, her feet carrying her toward the north side of the camp, where the bombs were falling.

The world around her was a nightmare of fire and smoke. Buildings had been reduced to rubble, tents torn apart by the blasts. People were running in every direction, desperate to escape the violence, but Yasmin only had one destination in mind. Her heart pounded in her chest, each step feeling like it took her further away from the safety she longed for.

As she approached the north side of the camp, the destruction became more apparent. The ground was littered with debris—shattered metal, broken glass, pieces of fabric that had once been part of someone's home. The air was thick with smoke, making it hard to breathe, and Yasmin's lungs burned as she pushed forward, her body trembling with fear and exhaustion.

"Please, Allah," she whispered, her voice shaking. "Please protect them. Please let them be safe."

The closer she got to their tent, the worse the devastation became. The bombs had fallen directly on the north side, flattening everything in their path. Tents had been reduced to ashes, and the sound of people crying for help filled the air, a haunting chorus of despair that echoed through Yasmin's heart.

When she reached the area where her family's tent had been, her breath caught in her throat.

There was nothing left. The tent, the small space that had become their home, was gone—obliterated by the bombs that had rained down from the sky. All that remained was rubble, a scattering of debris that stretched as far as the eye could see.

Yasmin's knees buckled beneath her, and she fell to the ground, her hands clawing at the dirt as she screamed.

"No!" Her voice was raw, broken, the sound of her heart shattering into a thousand pieces. "No! Muhammad! Hassan! Khaled!"

Her cries were swallowed by the chaos around her, but she couldn't stop, her body trembling as she searched frantically through the rubble, her hands shaking as she pushed aside pieces of debris. She felt like she was drowning, each breath harder to take than the last as she called out their names, her voice growing weaker with each passing moment.

"Please, please," she begged, her tears falling freely down her face as she dug through the remains of their tent. "Please, Allah, don't take them from me. Not them. Not now."

But no matter how much she prayed, no matter how hard she searched, the truth was inescapable. Her hands, scraped and bloodied from the rubble, finally came to rest on something soft. Her heart froze as she lifted a piece of fabric, revealing a familiar shape beneath the debris.

It was Muhammad.

His body lay still, half-buried beneath the rubble, his face peaceful in death. Yasmin's breath caught in her throat, her vision blurring as she collapsed beside him, her hands trembling as she touched his face, his skin already cold.

"No," she whispered, her voice breaking. "Muhammad, no. Please..."

But there was no response. Muhammad was gone. The man who had loved her, who had stood by her side through every hardship, had been taken from her in an instant, his life snuffed out by the violence of the war that had already claimed so much.

Yasmin's sobs wracked her body, her heart shattering as she clung to his lifeless form. "I'm so sorry," she whispered, her tears falling onto his chest. "I'm so sorry I wasn't here..."

Her world had come crashing down around her, the last pieces of her happiness ripped away in a single moment. But even as she wept over Muhammad's body, her heart clenched with a new fear.

Where were Hassan and Khaled?

Yasmin forced herself to stand, though her legs trembled beneath her. She wiped her tears, though more fell in their place, and she continued to search the rubble, her heart pounding with terror. **They had to be here. They had to be.**

But as the minutes stretched on, as her hands grew numb from the cold and her mind clouded with grief, she realized the truth. Her brothers were gone too.

She found them lying together beneath a collapsed beam, their small bodies still, their faces peaceful in death. Hassan, with his wide, curious eyes, and Khaled, who had always been the more playful of the two, now lay silent, their lives cut short by the war that had consumed everything.

Yasmin collapsed beside them, her heart too broken for words. Her sobs filled the air, her cries of grief rising above the smoke and fire that still lingered around her. She had lost everything—her father, Omar, her mother, and now Muhammad and her brothers. The world had taken everything from her, and now there was nothing left but her broken heart and the shattered remains of her family.

She didn't know how long she knelt there, her hands clutching the lifeless bodies of her brothers, her mind numb with grief. Time seemed to stretch, the minutes dragging on endlessly as she wept for the family she had lost. She prayed for them, prayed that Allah would grant them peace, even as her own heart screamed with the unfairness of it all.

How much more could she lose? How much more could she bear?

Eventually, the chaos around her began to fade, the sounds of the bombing replaced by the eerie silence of destruction. The social workers found her there, kneeling among the ruins, her body trembling with exhaustion and sorrow.

"Yasmin," Sarah whispered, her voice thick with emotion as she knelt beside her. "I'm so sorry."

Yasmin didn't respond, her eyes staring blankly ahead, her hands still clutching the lifeless form of her youngest brother.

"We need to get you out of here," Sarah said gently, placing a hand on Yasmin's shoulder. "It's not safe."

But Yasmin couldn't move. She couldn't leave them, couldn't let go of the only family she had left.

"Please, Yasmin," Sarah whispered, her voice breaking. "Come with us. We'll help you."

The words barely registered in Yasmin's mind, her grief too overwhelming to allow her to think clearly. But slowly, painfully, she let go of her brothers and stood, her body weak, her heart shattered.

She turned to Sarah, her voice barely a whisper. "They're gone," she said, her words heavy with the weight of her loss. "They're all gone."

Sarah nodded, her eyes filled with tears. "I know," she whispered. "I'm so sorry."

Yasmin followed Sarah out of the rubble, her heart numb, her mind blank. She had nothing left. No family, no home. The war had taken everything.

All she had now was her faith.

That night, as she lay beneath the cold, starless sky, Yasmin whispered a prayer to Allah. Her heart ached with the weight of her grief, but her words were filled with quiet acceptance.

"Please, Allah," she whispered. "Grant them peace. Take care of them, wherever they are."

The sky was silent, the world around her quiet, but Yasmin felt a sense of calm settle over her. She had lost everything, but she still had her faith.

And in that faith, she found the strength to keep going.

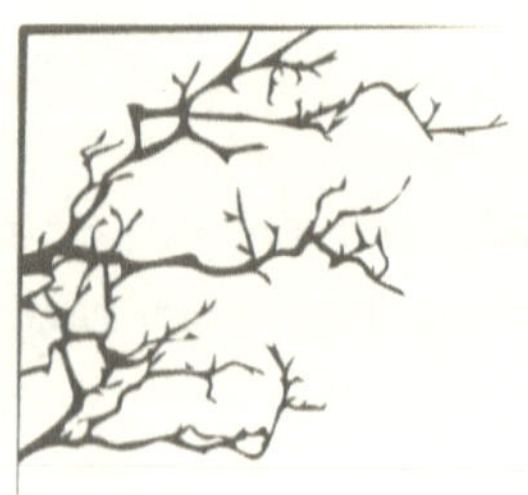

Chapter 11

Faith Unbroken

The days after the bombing of Rafah were like a blurred dream to Yasmin. Everything seemed both surreal and painfully real at the same time, as if her body moved on instinct while her heart and mind lagged behind, too shattered by grief to keep up. The world she had known was gone—her father, Omar, her mother, Muhammad, Hassan, and Khaled ,Aaliyah all taken from her, swallowed by the war that had ravaged Gaza for as long as she could remember. She had lost everything.

But in the quiet moments, when the initial shock faded and the sorrow felt as if it would consume her whole, Yasmin did something that surprised even herself: she turned to Allah.

The war had stripped her of all she held dear, and yet, in her darkest hour, she found herself clinging more tightly to her faith. It was as though, in the absence of everything else, Allah's presence became more profound, more tangible. Her prayers became her lifeline, the only connection she had left to something greater than the endless cycle of loss and suffering. She prayed for her family, asking Allah to grant them peace in the afterlife. She prayed for strength, for the will to keep moving forward, even when everything in her heart urged her to give in to despair.

The refugee camp was in ruins, the people still reeling from the attack. Bodies had been buried in shallow graves, their families mourning the dead in hushed, tearful whispers. It seemed that every corner of the camp held echoes of loss, and Yasmin could see the same haunted look in the eyes of the survivors that she knew was reflected in her own. They were all broken in some way, living in the shadows of what they had once been.

But they were still alive.

Yasmin had survived, and though her heart was heavy with grief, there was still a flicker of purpose deep inside her, something that refused to be extinguished. It was her faith that had kept her alive through the horrors of war, and it was that same faith that gave her the strength to rise from the ashes of her old life.

Weeks passed, and life in the camp continued, though in a diminished form. The tents were ragged, the food scarce, and the air thick with tension. Aid workers still came when they could, though the blockade and the constant fighting made it difficult for supplies to get through. Disease was rampant, and medical help was sparse at best. It was a place that had long since stopped feeling like a temporary refuge and more like a permanent prison, with each day blurring into the next, each new loss weighing down the spirits of those who remained.

Yet through it all, Yasmin found a new sense of purpose.

She had lost everything, yes—but she was still here. And in that simple truth, she found the strength to help others. There were so many people in the camp who were suffering just as much as she was—children who had lost their parents, mothers who had lost their sons, families torn apart by the war. And though Yasmin's heart ached with her own grief, she knew that she could not turn away from the suffering of others. Not when she understood it so intimately.

She began to spend her days volunteering with the aid workers, not just to distribute food and supplies but to offer comfort to those around her. She sat with mothers as they wept for their children, held the hands of the sick and injured, and listened to the stories of loss that mirrored her own. And though there were times when the pain of it all felt unbearable, Yasmin found that helping others, even in the smallest of ways, helped her to heal.

She had no family left, but in the camp, she found a new kind of family—a community of survivors who, like her, had nothing but their faith to hold onto. And together, they found strength in that shared faith, in the knowledge that no matter how much they had lost, Allah was with them.

One evening, as the sun set over the camp, casting the sky in shades of pink and gold, Yasmin sat with an elderly woman named Hala. Hala had lost her entire family in the bombing, her tent destroyed by the same blast that had killed Yasmin's brothers and husband. She was frail, her face lined with grief and age, but her spirit was strong.

"How do you keep going?" Hala asked, her voice quiet, almost lost in the gentle wind. "How do you still believe, after everything?"

BENEATH THE ASHES A TESTAMENT OF FAITH

Yasmin looked up at the sky, the fading light casting long shadows over the camp. It was a question she had asked herself many times since the war had begun, since the bombs had taken her family from her. But now, as she sat beside Hala, she felt a calmness settle over her.

"Because I have to," Yasmin replied softly. "If I lose my faith, then what do I have left? The war has taken everything from me, but it can't take my faith. That is something no one can take. Allah is with us, even in our suffering. I believe that. And I believe that we will find peace one day, in this life or the next."

Hala nodded slowly, her eyes filling with tears. "You're right," she whispered. "Allah is with us. He always has been."

Yasmin smiled, though her heart still ached with the weight of her losses. It wasn't an easy truth to hold onto, but it was the only truth that mattered. Her faith was what had kept her alive through all of this, and it was her faith that would carry her through whatever came next.

As the months passed, Yasmin became known throughout the camp as someone people could turn to in their time of need. She wasn't a healer, but her presence brought comfort to those who were suffering. She wasn't a leader, but her strength inspired others to keep going, even when the weight of their grief felt unbearable.

She spent her days caring for the children who had been orphaned by the war, helping to teach them, to guide them through the trauma that had become their reality. She sat with the elderly, listening to their stories of a Gaza that no longer existed, reminding them that they were still valued, still loved, despite everything they had lost.

Yasmin's own heart still carried the scars of her losses, but her faith had become a flame that could not be extinguished. Every morning, she rose to pray, her forehead pressed to the earth, her voice trembling as she asked Allah for strength, for guidance. And every night, as the stars twinkled overhead, she whispered her gratitude for another day of survival.

The war had taken her family, but it had not taken her faith. And in that faith, she had found a new kind of strength—a strength that allowed her to help others, to be a beacon of hope in a place that had long since forgotten what hope felt like.

The suffering in Palestine did not end. The war continued, the bombs still fell, and the people of Gaza remained trapped in a conflict that seemed to have no end. The world outside the camp moved on, but for those within its borders, life was a constant struggle for survival. The blockade continued to strangle the city, cutting off vital supplies of food, medicine, and fuel. The streets were filled with rubble, the homes reduced to ruins, and the children who had once laughed and played in the sunlight now wandered through the rubble, their eyes hollow with hunger and fear.

But even in the face of such overwhelming hardship, the people of Gaza remained resilient. They had no choice but to endure, to keep moving forward, one day at a time. And though the war had taken so much from them, it had not taken their faith.

For the people of Gaza, faith was more than just a belief—it was their lifeblood, the thing that kept them alive when everything else had been stripped away. It was the quiet prayers whispered in the dead of night, the hands raised in supplication, the hearts that turned to Allah for solace and strength. It was the one thing the war could not destroy.

Yasmin had come to understand this more deeply than ever before. She had seen so much suffering, had lost so many people she loved, and yet, her faith had only grown stronger. It had become the foundation of her life, the one thing she could cling to in a world that had been shattered by violence.

Every day, as she worked alongside the aid workers and cared for the people of the camp, Yasmin felt her connection to Allah deepening. She no longer asked why these things had happened to her—why she had lost her family, why the war had torn her life apart. She had come to accept that these were questions she would never have answers to. Instead, she focused on what she could do, on how she could serve others, and on how her faith could guide her through the darkness.

She had found a peace that transcended the chaos of the world around her—a peace that came from knowing that Allah was always with her, even in the midst of war. And with that peace came strength, a strength that allowed her to face each new day, no matter what it brought.

As the years passed, the war continued to rage, but Yasmin's resolve only grew stronger. She became a pillar of the community in the camp, a source of comfort and guidance for those who had lost their way. She had nothing left to give but her time, her compassion, and her faith, but for the people around her, that was more than enough.

She watched as new families arrived in the camp, their faces gaunt with fear, their hearts heavy with grief. She saw the children, wide-eyed and innocent, who had been born into a world of conflict and destruction, and she prayed for them every day, asking Allah to protect them, to grant them a future free from the horrors of war.

Yasmin had lost everything, but she had found something in return—something far more valuable than anything the war could take from her.

She had found peace in her faith.

And that faith, that unwavering belief in Allah's mercy and guidance, was the one thing that kept her alive. It was the thing that kept all of them alive.

For the people of Palestine, faith was not just a part of their lives—it was their survival. It was the thing that allowed them to endure the unimaginable, to keep moving forward, even when the world seemed determined to break them. It was the thing that kept their hearts beating, their spirits strong, even when everything else had been lost.

As Yasmin stood one evening, watching the sun set over the horizon, casting the sky in hues of orange and red, she whispered a prayer to Allah, her heart full of gratitude for the strength He had given her.

"Thank you, Allah," she whispered. "For everything. For the strength to keep going. For the faith that sustains us. For the hope that never fades."

And as the last rays of sunlight disappeared behind the clouds, Yasmin smiled—a small, peaceful smile that held within it the quiet resilience of a woman who had lost everything, yet found the most important thing of all.

Her faith.

It was the faith of the people of Palestine, the faith that had carried them through war, through loss, through unimaginable suffering. It was the faith that gave them the strength to endure, to fight for their lives, and to believe in a better future, even when that future seemed impossible.

The war had taken so much from them, but it had not taken their faith.

And as long as they had that faith, they would survive.

For faith in Allah was the one thing that could never be destroyed.

End.....

Don't miss out!

Visit the website below and you can sign up to receive emails whenever Nazreen zainab publishes a new book. There's no charge and no obligation.

https://books2read.com/r/B-A-NKTJC-YKXZE

Did you love *Beneath The Ashes A Testament of Faith*? Then you should read *Resilience In The Shadows*[1] by Nazreen zainab!

[2]

"Resilience in the Shadows"

Aaliya Yusuf, a devout Muslim and a woman of immense strength, is trapped in a nightmare marriage with a man who hides his cruelty behind a facade of piety. Subjected to severe abuse, including emotional torment, physical violence, Aaliya reaches a breaking point and makes the brave decision to escape, with the support of her loving family.

Free at last, Aaliyah embarks on a journey of healing and self-discovery, striving to rebuild her life for the sake of her two young sons. Just as she begins to find peace, Zayd Malik, a kind and devout man, enters her life. With his gentle demeanor and deep faith, Zayd helps Aaliyah rediscover the joys of love and laughter.

---

1. https://books2read.com/u/4AMJ8o

2. https://books2read.com/u/4AMJ8o

In "Resilience in the Shadows", Aaliyah 's story unfolds as one of courage, faith, and the transformative power of love. This emotionally gripping novel, rooted in Islamic values, is a testament to the strength of the human spirit and the possibility of finding light after darkness. Aaliyah 's journey is both heart-wrenching and inspiring, showing that even in the depths of despair, hope and healing are possible.

Also by Nazreen zainab

Deception in Bloom
Beneath The Ashes A Testament of Faith
Resilience In The Shadows